LOUDER THAN WORDS

KATHY KACER

annick press
toronto + berkeley

Annick Press Ltd.

We acknowledge the support of the Canada Council for the Arts and the
Ontario Arts Council, and the participation of the Government of Canada/
la participation du gouvernement du Canada for our publishing activities.

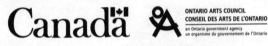

Canada

ONTARIO ARTS COUNCIL
CONSEIL DES ARTS DE L'ONTARIO
an Ontario government agency
un organisme du gouvernement de l'Ontario

Library and Archives Canada Cataloguing in Publication

Title: Louder than words / Kathy Kacer.
Names: Kacer, Kathy, 1954- author.
Series: Kacer, Kathy, 1954- Heroes quartet.
Description: Series statement: Heroes quartet
Identifiers: Canadiana (print) 20190185422 | Canadiana (ebook)
20190185430 | ISBN 9781773213552
   (hardcover) | ISBN 9781773213545 (softcover) | ISBN 9781773213583
(PDF) | ISBN 9781773213569
   (EPUB) | ISBN 9781773213576 (Kindle) | ISBN 9781773213576
Classification: LCC PS8571.A33 L69 2020 | DDC jC813/.54—dc23

Published in the U.S.A. by Annick Press (U.S.) Ltd.
Distributed in Canada by University of Toronto Press.
Distributed in the U.S.A. by Publishers Group West.

Printed in Canada

www.annickpress.com
kathykacer.com

Also available in e-book format. Please visit www.annickpress.com/ebooks.html
for more details.

For Ian, always by my side.

—K.K.

Whoever saves one life saves the world entire.

—FROM THE TALMUD AND THE QURAN

PROLOGUE

September 1941

"Open up! We need to search the house!"

I locked eyes with Nina as the pounding at the door began. Her face was so pale you could almost see through her skin. My sister Nadia said nothing. Only her stillness gave away the fear she must have been feeling. She was only six but had become so grown-up in the last months—no longer a child. Even my baby sister Galya had stopped moving, and sat quiet and wide-eyed in her high chair. She wasn't a crier, and she could barely talk, thank goodness—couldn't ask or answer any questions.

"Open up, now!"

"Let me do the talking," Nina said as she rose from the table, wrapped her shawl firmly around her shoulders, and went to open the door. Three soldiers in uniform pushed past her into the house.

They wore gray jackets cinched at the waist with thick black belts, and tall black leather boots that clomped across the floor. One soldier walked into the bedroom and a second to the kitchen. The tallest of the three did the talking.

"We've had a report that you may be harboring Jews here," he said. He had a neck as thick as a tree trunk and a round belly that jammed up against the buttons of his jacket, threatening to push through.

"You can see that there's no one here other than the four of us," Nina replied. I marveled at how calm she sounded.

I stood beside Nadia in a corner of the room. My legs felt so weak that for a moment I was afraid I might fall down. I commanded my body to stop shaking while I leaned in to my sister for support. She looked up at me, and that was when her face froze, her eyes dropping to my chest, and to the Star of David on its thin gold chain that still hung around my neck. My star! The one Mama had given to me before she disappeared. I always remembered to take it off every morning and put it under my pillow, just as she had instructed. Today, for some reason, I had forgotten.

My stomach dropped. Quickly, I raised my hand

and slipped the star under my blouse, all the while praying that the soldier with the thick neck hadn't seen me. He was still talking to Nina.

"We'll search for ourselves and see what we can find."

From the bedroom, I heard one soldier moving furniture and overturning the contents of drawers. The one in the kitchen was opening cupboard doors, pulling things from inside, and dumping them on the floor. The one who did the talking hadn't moved. He stood staring first at Nina, and then at me and Nadia. The baby was still silent, as if she sensed the danger around her.

I stared down at the wooden floor and noticed a spider creeping its way across, falling into the small ruts and grooves between the wooden planks and then reappearing, regaining its balance, and moving forward again. Silently, I rooted for the spider, hoping it would make its way across the floor and into the safety of the wall on the other side.

The soldier spoke again. "Is there no one else who lives here?" He thrust out his round belly even more and took a step closer to Nina.

As he did so, the spider crept into his path. Any second now, his boot would squish it.

I gasped, and the soldier stopped in his tracks,

turning his head to look at me.

I ran a shaky hand through my short hair and then shoved my trembling fist into the pocket of my skirt.

The soldier stared.

I lowered my eyes.

My star pressed against my chest.

The soldier came toward me.

The spider kept walking.

CHAPTER 1

Six Months Earlier

It was a cold day in February when Nina came to live with us. The snow had fallen so hard overnight that school was cancelled. We didn't get many breaks from school, so I looked forward to a day off and the chance to play with my little sisters in the backyard.

I was twelve years old, but people always told me I looked and acted older. Maybe it was my serious expression, or the way I listened when grown-ups talked. Or maybe it was having younger siblings to help care for. Mama said it was as if my mind was at least sixteen when my body was still a younger girl. I liked that, liked the thought that I was more mature than I looked. It meant that people often treated me as if I were an adult, and I liked that too.

Mama had been telling us for some time that we needed a housekeeper—practically since Papa had died a year earlier. He had been a literature teacher at the local high school. Mama was going to take over his job and return to work full-time.

"The savings that your papa put aside won't last for much longer. I'm lucky to get the work," she said. It was true: she hadn't been a teacher for many years. But it meant that she would be away from the house all day. That was why we needed a housekeeper.

I knew that we needed someone else here at home to make Mama's life easier—and probably mine as well. But I couldn't bear the idea of someone I didn't know coming to live with us. It was hard enough getting used to life without Papa.

Sometimes I still couldn't believe he was gone, even though I had watched him getting sicker by the day. He had become more tired than usual. I would catch him slumped over at the kitchen table, his fists clenched. But when I asked what was wrong, he would always tell me it was nothing serious. "Just the usual small pain here," he would say, pointing to his chest. Then he'd smile and ask me to make tea. Mama admitted to me that Papa's heart was weak. She said that we shouldn't burden him too much with our concerns because that would only make his heart weaker. So I never told him how worried I was about his health. But I noticed that he stopped throwing baby Galya into the air and catching her as she squealed with delight, and that he stopped carrying Nadia around on his back while she begged him to gallop like a horse. And then he took to his bed, and then he died. It happened so fast. He was awake when I left for school one day, and gone by the time I came home.

"But I wasn't here to say goodbye," I sobbed.

"Papa knew how much you loved him," Mama said between her tears.

That didn't make me feel much better. Papa's heart may have been sick, but mine felt as if it was broken. I cried and cried until there were no more tears inside of me. There was a picture of Papa that hung in our sitting room over the fireplace. I looked at it now, wishing once more that he was still with us.

"Dina, I can't work and look after the house as well as the three of you," Mama said, interrupting my thoughts. "I need help."

I carried the plates to the sink, avoiding Mama's eyes. "I can help," I protested, as I always did. "I don't need anyone to look after me. And I can take care of my sisters." I was already changing the baby's diapers and helping Nadia get dressed for school. I could cook and clean without anyone watching over me.

"And what's the baby supposed to do when you and Nadia are at school? Will she look after herself?" Mama walked over to me, turned me around by the shoulders, and lifted my chin. "My job starts this week. We have no choice."

"But who is this person?"

"She's a very experienced housekeeper. She isn't married, but she's worked for many families and looked after many children. Someone at the school knew of her and gave me her name."

"But she's a stranger."

Mama sighed. "That may be, but there isn't anyone else who can be here all day while I'm at work. She's arriving today. So, I'm afraid you're going to have to get used to having her here, my darling. It's either this, or we starve."

I was playing outside with Nadia when Mama called us in. We were trying to make a giant ball of snow and not having much luck. The snow was too light and feathery, not the wet and sticky kind that we needed. Our giant ball looked more like a pointy hill. Still, it made Nadia laugh until she fell down into the snow and rolled over and over. When she stood up, she looked more like a ball of snow than the mound we had piled together.

"Eldina, Gennadiy," Mama called, poking her head out the back door and pulling her shawl up to her neck to protect against the cold and wind. "Come inside. I want you to meet someone."

She only called us by our proper names when it was really important. I knew what this was about, and I walked toward the house as slow as a turtle, dragging my feet the whole way. Nadia followed. Maybe if I walked slowly enough, the stranger would grow impatient and leave.

We came into the kitchen, brushing snow off our coats and removing our boots by the back door. That was when I came face-to-face with Nina for the first time. She was as small as she was wide, standing half a head shorter than me. She wore a simple long skirt and flowered cotton blouse, and a bright red scarf was wrapped tightly around her head and tied under her chin. Her skin was worn and lined, like old leather. She had a deep dimple only on one side of her face. It disappeared, like a crater, into the folds of her skin. I had no way of knowing how old she was. Twenty? Forty? A hundred?

As she walked toward me, I shrank back; she looked more like a troll than someone I wanted to meet. But then she smiled and her dimple deepened, and her eyes crinkled at the corners and twinkled like two stars in the sky at night. Her grin was so wide it threatened to push past her ears.

"This is Mrs. Pukas," Mama said. "Say hello to her."

There was a small silver cross suspended from a thin chain that hung around Nina's neck. Mama had already told me that the new housekeeper was Catholic. That didn't surprise me. There were many Catholic people living and working in our community.

I dropped my eyes and curtsied the way Mama had taught me to do with elders.

Nina extended her hand and I took it. It was chapped and rough, as if it had been soaking in harsh laundry soap for years. But her voice, when she spoke, was soft and cheery.

"It's lovely to meet you," she said. "What is your name?"

"Eldina," I replied.

"What a pretty name!"

"But everyone calls me Dina."

"And you may call me Nina," she said.

"Oh no," Mama interrupted. "It's too familiar."

"But I insist," Nina said. She stared right at me. "If we're to be friends, then we should know one another by our first names."

I didn't want to be friends with this woman! But I smiled politely.

"So, I am Nina and you are Dina," she continued.

"Your names rhyme!" Nadia exclaimed.

I had noticed that too, but hadn't wanted to say it out loud.

"Imagine that!" Nina replied. "That means that we're friends already." She looked at Mama as she said this. "Is it all right with you, Mrs. Sternik? First names are so much easier."

Mama sighed. "Yes, I suppose it's fine."

Nina bent to look at my sister, who was half-hidden behind me. "And what is your name?" she asked. "I hope we can be friends too."

"Her name is Gennadiy. But we call her Nadia," Mama replied.

"She's six," I added.

"Six and a half," Nadia declared, stepping out from behind me.

Nina smiled again. "Six and a half is a very important age."

"I like your scarf," Nadia said.

Nina reached up to touch her head. "I have lots of these—in many different colors. You'll never lose sight of me in a crowd. And who is this one?" Nina pointed at Galya, seated in her high chair and sucking her thumb contentedly.

"Her name is Galya, but we usually just call her the baby," I explained.

"And are you a good sister to these two?"

I paused at that. It was something I'd never been asked before.

"She's my best friend," Nadia whispered.

"And very loving to the baby," Mama added.

"Then you are very good to them indeed," Nina said. I felt my cheeks redden.

"I really must get to work," Mama said, pulling on her wool coat and boots, and wrapping a scarf around her head and neck. "I'm only going in for a couple of hours today." She glanced out the window where the snow was still falling in powdery clusters. "There won't be any classes, but I'm hoping to sit down with some of the other teachers." She looked over at me. "And it will give you a chance to get to know one another." Then she gave Nina some instructions for dinner and looking after the baby. Finally, she came over to me and bent to give me a hug. "Please try," she whispered into my ear. "Be patient with Nina. You must understand why this is necessary."

I wanted to please Mama and I wanted to accept this new person. But I wasn't sure I was ready for any of that. I hugged my mother back but made no reply.

At the door, Mama turned back to Nina. "Please be careful if you leave the house. You never know who might be around."

Nina's brow creased. "Is it dangerous for the children?"

"I'm probably being too cautious," Mama said. "But lately I've heard of Jewish people being harassed on the streets. I don't want any trouble."

"I'll be very careful," Nina said to Mama. "I won't let the children out of my sight."

CHAPTER 2

As soon as Mama left, Nina set to work chopping vegetables for that night's supper.

"I'm going to take Nadia and the baby outside to play," I announced.

Nina's eyes grew round with fear. "Your mother said not to go out."

I frowned. Hadn't she noticed that I'd been outside when she arrived? "Mama didn't mean not to go into the yard," I said, trying to keep the irritation out of my voice. "The yard has a fence around it. Mama meant not to go into the city."

Our city, Proskurov, had changed borders so many times over the years that it was hard to keep up with its history. It had once been part of the kingdom of Poland, then part of Russia, and now it was a part of Soviet Ukraine. Papa had always said that it was amazing how many armies had fought over this small piece of land—*hardly worth all the fuss*, he had said. But lately, it seemed that my country was in the middle of a battle for control once again.

Much of it was because of that man, Adolf Hitler, the leader of Germany to the west of my country. He and his Nazi army were at war with Poland and other countries, and a lot of his hostility was directed at the Jewish citizens of Europe. And then there was the leader of Russia to the east of us, Joseph Stalin. He was opposed to Hitler, but he hated Jewish people almost as much as Hitler did. There were laws in other countries about what Jewish people could and couldn't do, where they could work, where they could shop, and who they could be friends with. We didn't have those laws in my city, and Mama insisted they wouldn't come to pass. Still, there was a long history in my country of Jewish people being mistreated and persecuted. Recently, we had heard a terrifying report that Hitler's armies had moved into Ukraine, taking over cities in the west like Sambir, Horodok, and Busk. Those places were still some distance from Proskurov. But if Hitler could conquer them, would our city be next? Nothing had happened to us here—not yet, at least. But there had been incidents, small ones, directed against Jews. You never knew when someone might throw a terrible insult your way, like when Ivan, a boy in my class, yelled at my best friend, Esther, *Jews have no brains*. That's the kind of thing Mama really meant when she told Nina to watch us carefully.

As I put on my coat, I could tell that Nina was worried.

"I play in the yard all the time," I reassured her. "I'm very responsible. Besides, no one is around."

That part was true. Our house was some distance from our neighbors, and while we could walk to the city center, it felt as if we lived in the country, surrounded by tall trees and open spaces.

Nina sighed. "Yes, well, okay. Just please stay close by where I can keep an eye on you."

"You'll be able to see us out the window," I said, even though I knew that no one needed to watch out for me, least of all this new stranger who thought I needed to be looked after the way the baby did. Nadia already had her coat on. I helped her with her boots, and then scooped Galya into my arms after dressing her in a jacket and tying her wool hat securely under her chin.

Outside, the snow was still falling in soft waves. The baby tilted her head back and opened her mouth to catch some flakes. Nadia headed for a pile of stones that lay in one corner of the garden. She brushed the snow off the top of the pile and sank down in front of it. Nadia was a collector. She gathered things and kept them in her room in special places that she assigned for each collection. For a while, she had collected pieces of glass. Then it was ribbons. Lately, she had been collecting stones.

"Come see, Dina," she called.

I set the baby down in the snow and walked over to Nadia. The stones in her pile were every shape, size, and color imaginable. Some were flat and smooth; others were round; still others were rough and jagged. She held up one that was nearly as blue as the sky on a sunny day.

"Do you like it?" she asked. "I found it next to the house."

"It's pretty," I said. "But what are you going to do with all the stones? You can't bring them into the house. Mama would never allow it."

Nadia shared her room with the baby, and it was becoming quite a mess, piled with mounds of collectables that she had amassed over the years; *treasures*, she called them. Thank goodness, I had a room to myself. Mine was the smallest room in the house— really just enough space for my bed and one chest of drawers. But I didn't care that the room was tiny, as long as I had my privacy.

"These are my *outside* treasures. But Mama said I could pick a few to keep inside. This one, for sure." Nadia slipped the blue stone into the pocket of her jacket and then leaned over to play with the others, trying to set them on top of one another in a tower. I turned back to the baby, grabbing her just as she was about to shove a handful of snow into her mouth. There was a wooden swing suspended from the giant oak tree that towered over our home in the yard. After brushing snow from its seat, I sat down with Galya in my lap and began to pump my legs forward and backward, hanging onto her with one hand and the rope with the other. She squealed with joy.

By the time we went back inside, it was just beginning to grow dark. My cheeks had turned bright red, and my fingers tingled from the cold. The house smelled of onions. There was a fire roaring in the fireplace, and the floor had been polished to a bright shine.

"I was just about to call you in," Nina said. "I'm making *varenyky*."

How could she know that was my favorite? Those dumplings stuffed with potatoes were heavenly. Mama liked fried onions on top of hers, but I loved to slather mine with sour cream. The hot and cold flavors rolling around my mouth was an indescribably delicious combination. Was Nina trying to win me over with my favorite foods?

"Your mother will be home soon, and I want to have everything ready for supper," Nina continued. "Would you like to help?"

I nodded. Nadia went off to add her blue stone to her "inside" collection, while I put the baby in her high chair and set the table for dinner, just as our old grandfather clock chimed six times. The clock had been a gift from Mama's mother, whom I had never known. She died before I was born. Mama loved that clock. She polished its dark mahogany wood every week, sometimes twice a week. She said that she could speak to her mother while she was polishing. The weighted pendulum inside the tower swung back and forth ticking away the seconds. Mama said that was like listening to her mother's heartbeat. And when the bells celebrated the arrival of each hour with a chorus of chimes, Mama said it was as if her mother was singing to her.

"What a good job you're doing," Nina commented as I moved around the table.

What did she think? Of course, I was doing a good job. I had been setting the table since I was Nadia's age.

"But of course, you know exactly how to set a table, don't you?" she added. It was as if she was reading my mind.

I smiled at the compliment. Then I glanced over at Papa's picture on the wall. Just like Mama, he would have told me to be patient; give Nina a chance. I wasn't ready to be her friend. But I had to admit, she was nice.

CHAPTER 3

I woke up the next morning to a soft knock on my bedroom door and knew instantly that it had to be Nina. Mama's knock wasn't so gentle. When I opened one eye, sunlight was pouring in from the window next to my bed. It looked as if the snow had stopped overnight.

I stretched and sat up, rubbing the sleep from my eyes. "Come in."

The door opened with a soft creak and Nina's face appeared on the other side—the same wrinkled and craggy cheeks softened by her big wide smile. She had changed the scarf she was wearing around her head. Today it was bright yellow.

"Good morning, Dina," she said. Her voice was as cheery as it had sounded the day before. "It's time to get up and get ready for school."

"Already?" I asked, brushing the hair back off my face. It felt as if only minutes had passed since I'd gone to bed. "Where's Mama?"

"She had to leave early for work." Nina moved toward my closet. "I'm going to walk with you and the little ones, just so I know where your school is—and to let the baby get some fresh air. Would you like me to pick your clothes for you?"

I frowned. It was one thing for Nina to walk us all to school. But Mama had stopped choosing my clothes years ago. Nina caught my look.

"Oh, but what am I saying? Of course, you're old enough to do that for yourself. I'll go help the little ones." She smiled that smile that stretched across her face, and I nodded.

I dressed, and before leaving my bedroom, I paused to look at myself in front of the small mirror that hung above my dresser drawer. I smoothed down the collar of my blouse, trying to conceal the edge that had begun to fray. These days, Mama had less money to buy new clothes for any of us. Her first worry was keeping food on the table. I wondered briefly what my friend Esther would be wearing today. She was always dressed in the latest fashion. Esther's father was a tailor. He made suits for most of the men from our Jewish community, and even some officials in the county office. But he could also fashion women's clothing with no patterns and nothing to guide him *except his imagination.* That's what Esther was always telling me. He made all of her dresses.

I turned my head from side to side and then brushed my short blond curls off my forehead and into a small clip on one side. When Mama had told me about the laws in other countries forbidding Jewish people to do this and that, she had also said that one of the ways the authorities could tell whether or not you were Jewish was by your appearance. Those with dark hair and prominent noses were singled out before others. Why did everyone think that all Jewish people had dark hair, dark eyes, and big noses? Mama had dark hair and eyes, but she was the only one in our family who did. My hair was as yellow as a pale sun. And my eyes were as blue as the stone Nadia had found next to the house. My sisters were fair-haired and fair-skinned too, like Papa had been.

Satisfied with how my hair looked, I smoothed down my skirt and walked into the kitchen, surprised to see Nadia and the baby already eating breakfast. Usually, it was my job to help them get ready in the morning.

"You'd better be quick," Nina said, pouring me a cup of tea and placing the basket of warm bread next to my plate. I smiled at her, grateful that she had organized the younger ones. I tickled the baby under her chin and then grabbed a slice of bread, slathered it with jam, and gulped it down along with my tea. Then we bundled ourselves up and set off for the walk to school.

Proskurov was a pretty city. It sat next to the Bug River, which wound lazily through town, twisting and snaking like a caterpillar zigzagging its way between blades of grass. The river cozied up to small parks along its banks and curved under wooden bridges. This morning, the air was cold and I could see my breath in front of my face. I walked as quickly as I could through the deep snow, careful to stay several steps ahead of Nina and my sisters. I didn't want anyone to think I needed a babysitter to walk me to school. Besides, I knew what it was like to walk with Nadia in the morning, since I was the one who usually did. She was slow, and always needed urging on. So as Nadia dawdled, her eyes searching the ground for stones buried in the snow, Nina pulled her along by one hand and pushed the baby carriage with the other.

We passed the market in the center of the city by Kamenetsky Street. This was the place where, twenty years ago, thousands of Jewish people had been killed by groups of soldiers from the Ukraine army. It happened before anyone knew what was going on—like *thunder on a clear day,* Papa had said. These days, Mama shopped here for groceries every week. Many of the vendors were still Jewish. This morning, they had already cleaned the snow from in front of their stalls and opened up, likely hours earlier. They were beginning to serve young mothers who were shopping for vegetables and meat, holding their babies in one arm and their shopping baskets in the other. Walking through the market today, it was hard to believe that such a terrible massacre had once happened here.

We paused to let the city tram move past us before dashing across the road, avoiding the cars that honked their horns to let us know they were coming. I had been on the tram only a couple of times in my whole life—once as a special treat, and once when we rode it to the cemetery on the outskirts of the city for Papa's funeral—two experiences that couldn't have been more different. Other than that, every place we needed to go was within walking distance of our home.

Next, we passed the library. Papa had been the one to take me here nearly every week. I'd barely had time to go since he was gone, and I missed it terribly.

Mrs. Timko was already outside her candy store, a basket in one hand. There was always a smile on Mrs. Timko's face, and she often sang when customers passed by. She was the happiest person I knew. And why not? She owned a candy shop with the most wonderful sweets in all of Proskurov. And she always had candies to pass out to any child who walked by. That would make anyone happy.

"Good morning, Mrs. Timko." I reached into her basket and grabbed the one I usually took, a square candy wrapped in silver foil. I knew it was chocolate, my favorite.

"Good morning, Eldina," she sang out to me as I thanked her. She always called me by my full name. "How are you on this glorious morning?"

I stifled a giggle, pulling my hat further down on my head. It was freezing cold outside, and only Mrs. Timko could see this day as beautiful. "I'm fine, thank you," I replied.

She looked curiously at Nina, who had caught up to me. "And who is this?"

I introduced our new housekeeper, explaining that she had come to look after me and my sisters since Mama was returning to work. "But mostly my sisters," I added.

Nina murmured, "Good morning."

Mrs. Timko's eyes took in Nina's bright yellow scarf, and then dropped to the cross that Nina wore around her neck. "Are you from this area?" she asked, smiling broadly. "I don't believe I've ever seen you before."

"I'm from the west," Nina said politely.

"And will you stay for long?"

"As long as the Sternik family needs me."

"Ah, yes," Mrs. Timko said, turning back to me. "Your mother has to deal with so much. But the Lord never gives us more than we can handle."

Mrs. Timko was a devout churchgoing woman who was always talking about what the Lord did and didn't do for us. She crossed herself and looked up to the sky as if she was waiting for someone or something to answer her. Then she looked back at Nina.

"If you'd like to come to church with me one Sunday, I'd be happy to bring you along."

"Thank you for the offer," Nina replied. "But I'll probably be busy helping Mrs. Sternik."

Mrs. Timko frowned. "Even on Sundays?"

"Well, perhaps one day," Nina said. "We'll see."

"Help yourself to a chocolate," Mrs. Timko added, thrusting her basket out to Nina. "I have enough here for everyone."

Nina reached into the basket and picked a candy,

then put it into her jacket pocket. "For later," she said, adding her thanks.

"I hope you're helping your mother and this lovely lady out," Mrs. Timko said to me as more children pressed up to her, reaching into her basket for sweets.

"She's the best helper anyone could ask for," Nina said. I felt my cheeks grow warm. "She seems very nice," Nina added as we walked on.

As soon as our school building came into sight, I turned to Nina. "I'm okay on my own from here." I pointed around the corner to where she needed to take Nadia. "That's where the class for the younger children is." I hoped Nina wouldn't walk me all the way to my class. But she just smiled and tightened her grip on my sister's hand.

"I'll be back later for Nadia," she said. "I know you can walk home on your own."

My face burned again when she said that.

"But perhaps you'll walk along with me and the little ones."

I shrugged, then turned and ran toward the playground, where I saw Esther waiting for me close to the school's outer gate. Today Esther was wearing a beautiful bright red coat and matching hat—something her father must have just made her. I looked enviously at the stylish fashion and sighed. I knew I shouldn't complain, and I never did in front of Mama. But a new dress from time to time would have been nice.

"Who's that?" Esther pointed to Nina, who was walking around the building with Nadia and the baby.

I explained who Nina was. "She's not really here for me," I added. "It's more for my sisters." I must have said that ten times by now. But Esther seemed satisfied.

Esther and I had only been friends for a couple of years. We met after her family moved to Proskurov from Felshtin, a city some distance away. Esther's father had moved his tailoring business to our town to take the place of Mr. Rabinovich, the aging tailor of our community who had retired a few years earlier.

"Did you get the homework done?" Esther asked, opening the book bag she was carrying. "I tried to write a story about what I want to do when I'm older, but I'm not sure it's any good. The words just don't come together for me. Will you take a look at it?" she asked, handing me the notebook she'd fished out of her bag.

I scanned Esther's homework. She had written about wanting to be a nurse, mostly taking care of elderly people. The story was good enough, but her writing was simple and needed something to make it more interesting.

"Why don't you talk about the work you did last summer helping out in the hospital? You could write about that old man who you helped get out of his wheelchair and walking."

Esther sighed. "I completely forgot about that! That's why I need you," she added. "Your mind is so creative and interesting. Mine is pretty dull."

"You don't read enough," I said. "That's your problem. You're good at history and math. But you can get so many ideas about writing from reading books."

Just then, some kind of commotion broke out across the schoolyard. Students began running toward a group that was circling something or someone; we couldn't tell what. And the kids in the middle were chanting something. It was only when Esther and I came closer that we could hear what was being said.

"Stinky Jews. Like stinky cheese."

The chant had started with only a few of the children gathered. But by the time Esther and I got there, others had joined in. Esther grabbed my arm. Her face was pale.

"Come on," she said. "We shouldn't be near this."

I knew she was probably right, but I needed to see

what was happening. Standing on my tiptoes, I could just make out the top of Ivan's head. He was the same boy who had taunted Esther weeks earlier, telling her that Jews had no brains. Ivan had never been much of a bully. He had always pretty much kept to himself, didn't have many friends, and never made any trouble—until recently. First Esther and now this. He was the one leading the chant in the middle of the ring, and urging others to chime in. Esther tugged on my arm again, but I shook her free and dove into the mob. Who was in the middle of the pack? Who was Ivan bullying?

It was Avrum, another boy from my class, a quiet student and pretty small for his age. He was on the ground, his arms up, trying to protect himself from Ivan and the rest of the gang. It didn't take much nerve to pick on the smallest person in class, I thought. I glared at Ivan and then searched the crowd for help.

Sure enough, I could see our teacher, Mr. Petrenko, limping unsteadily across the schoolyard toward the crowd. Mr. Petrenko had one lame leg, which he always swung out in a wide semicircle to join the other as he walked. No one knew why or how it had happened—if it was an injury or something he had been born with. He often used a cane, espe-

cially out on the playground. But not today. Today he
hobbled, unassisted but steadily, toward the commotion. *Finally*, I thought with relief. A few weeks earlier
there had been a schoolyard fight between two boys
who were known to be troublemakers. Mr. Petrenko
had charged right in to break it up.

But as he neared the crowd, Mr. Petrenko suddenly slowed to a stop, just outside the throng. I pushed
my way through and ran over to him.

"Please help," I said, my voice shaking with emo-
tion. The chanting behind me was getting louder.

Mr. Petrenko stared at me for a moment, shifting
unsteadily from one leg to the other and making no
move to do anything.

Maybe he couldn't hear what they were saying.
"That's Avrum in the middle of all that," I explained.
"You have to help him!"

At that, Mr. Petrenko shook his head and stammered, "You all need to work out your ... your dis-
agreements on your own."

I couldn't believe what he was saying. Didn't he
understand how serious this was? "They're beating
Avrum up!" I cried.

"I can't fix every problem that comes up," Mr.
Petrenko replied, looking at the group of students
once more and then turning away—but not before

I caught the look of embarrassment in his eyes. I couldn't understand it. But I realized in that moment that no one was going to do anything to help. Even the other Jewish students in my class had backed away, including Esther, as if they were all worried that they might be targeted next if they said or did anything.

I had to act. I turned back to the crowd and grabbed Esther's hand, thinking there had to be safety in numbers. She stiffened and pulled back, but I held on tight and dove into the center of the circle, coming face-to-face with Ivan, who was still pumping his arms in the air and leading everyone in his chant as though conducting a choir.

"Stinky Jews. Like stinky cheese."

"Stop it!" I commanded.

Ivan took a step closer to me, yelling into my face. "Stinky Jews. Like stinky cheese. Stinky Jews. Like stinky cheese."

My heart was thumping in my chest. I had placed myself in the middle of something that I might not be able to handle. Esther tugged on my arm, trying to pull me away. But somehow, despite the danger, I felt that I couldn't back down. I stood my ground and faced Ivan. "I said stop it!" I ordered again, this time at the top of my lungs.

It was as if I'd snapped him out of some kind of spell. Ivan stopped repeating that terrible chant, and his arm dropped down out of the air and back by his side. And when he stopped, the chanting around him died off as well. There was complete silence. My heart pounded like a drum. I had challenged Ivan and somehow shut him down. But now I was terrified he'd turn his bullying and the crowd against me. We stared at one another. And then, Ivan took a step toward me, a sharp glint in his eye. The crowd around us started murmuring again. Just as Ivan was raising his arm once more, Mr. Petrenko broke through the crowd and put a firm hand on Ivan's shoulder.

"Okay, everyone. It's time to get to class."

Too little, too late, I thought. Ivan glanced up at Mr. Petrenko and then looked over at me, as if he might say something more. But instead, he turned and marched out of the group and toward the school building. The rest of the crowd disbanded within seconds.

Mr. Petrenko looked at me. "Please go inside, Eldina," he said. His voice shook a bit, and he sounded almost sorry for what had happened. That confused me even more. Before walking away, he bent to help Avrum to his feet. Then he turned and limped after the others, swinging his lame leg at a furious pace.

Esther walked over to Avrum. "Are you okay?" she asked.

He nodded. His face was pale except for one bright circle of red high up on his cheek where Ivan must have struck him.

"It's good you came along," he said.

My heart rate was slowly returning to normal. "Ivan is usually all talk," I said, trying to keep my voice even. "You know that."

Avrum nodded, reaching up to rub his cheek. "He used to be all talk. But not today."

CHAPTER 4

Nina was in front of the school building when class was dismissed for the day. Nadia was right by her side, and the baby was tucked into the carriage and fast asleep. I hugged Nadia, mumbled a quick hello to Nina, and we set off for home. Nina pulled Nadia and the baby carriage along. I could see that she was being careful to stay a few steps behind me—not wanting to invade the space I had set up for myself. I appreciated that, especially today. But soon, they began to fall farther and farther behind, with Nadia stopping every few steps to search for stones. At this rate, we'd never get home, and I had little patience today. I stopped and waited for them to catch up.

"Do you want me to take the carriage?" I asked, and Nina nodded gratefully. While I pushed the carriage, Nadia chattered away about school, and for once I was glad not to have to make conversation.

"Is everything okay, Dina?" Nina asked at one point. "You're very quiet."

I nodded. My mind was still swirling over the events of that morning in the playground. Ivan had kept to himself for the rest of the day. And Mr. Petrenko didn't say another word about any of it. But I was confused and upset about why he hadn't stepped in sooner to stop Ivan from tormenting Avrum. I didn't want to confide any of this to Nina; I didn't know her well enough, and I didn't want to share something so troubling and personal. And besides, how could she possibly understand what it felt like to be taunted because of our religion? Mama was the one I wanted to talk to. She would help me understand what was going on. She would make me feel better about the whole thing.

As soon as we arrived home, I immediately began to set the table for dinner while Nina cooked and Nadia played with the baby. I couldn't wait for Mama to get home. But I wasn't the only one who wanted to talk to her. As soon as she walked in the door, Nadia threw herself into Mama's arms and launched into the same description of her day that she had talked about on our way home.

"We colored all morning and then we did some

reading. I read five whole pages in my book and I even read two pages out loud when the teacher asked me to. And then my friend Ilana asked if I would share my sandwich with her, but I didn't want to share and she said I was being selfish, but I didn't care because I wanted to eat the whole thing ..." On and on the stories went while Mama listened patiently through dinner. At one point she turned to look at me.

"You're very quiet this evening, my darling. Everything okay?"

At first, I just nodded. Nina looked up at me but didn't say a word. I stared back at Mama. "I have something I need to talk to you about," I said. "But I'll wait until later."

She frowned, but didn't say anything more—just turned back to Nadia, who continued to chatter away.

It was only after my sisters were put to bed, and Nina was busy cleaning up in the kitchen, that Mama and I were able to have a real conversation, one I could be sure wouldn't be overheard. And then I told her everything about the incident at school—Ivan tormenting Avrum, the chanting of that terrible line, me standing up to Ivan, and Mr. Petrenko doing nothing.

"These days, you have to be so careful when you challenge those bullies," Mama began, her forehead creased with worry.

"I know how to deal with someone like Ivan," I said. "He's really a coward. As soon as you confront him, he backs down. But Mr. Petrenko wouldn't help, even after I asked him to."

Mama's face grew pale. "You asked him for help?"

I nodded. "It was strange. He looked like he wanted to do something, and he helped Avrum off the ground when it was over. But when it really counted, he didn't do a thing."

All the while I was talking, I was aware of Nina moving silently through the kitchen. She was washing the dishes and then sweeping the floor. But I felt as though she was listening to every word I was saying, and it made me uncomfortable. What did she think about Mr. Petrenko and Ivan? Did she agree with what they had done? Maybe it was terrible of me to think that she might, but how could I know? I hardly knew her and didn't know if I could trust her. I had thought I could trust Mr. Petrenko, but he hadn't helped at all.

"Bullies like Ivan are weak," Mama agreed. "Perhaps it's best to ignore him."

"That's what I usually do. But I couldn't ignore what was happening to Avrum, could I?"

Mama sighed and shook her head. "You're such a good person, my darling. And brave to stand up for your friend." Mama looked worried as she said this. She leaned toward me and reached out to place her hand on my arm.

"I'm okay, Mama," I said.

"You're so grown up for your age. But maybe ..." She paused.

"What is it?" I felt as if she was keeping something from me. "Is something else wrong?"

Mama pulled her hand back. "It's just ..." She paused again, and this time, I was the one to reach out and take her arm.

"You have to tell me what's happening, Mama. Please."

Mama looked down and then away, and then back up to stare into my eyes. She took a deep breath. "I've heard of some ... incidents lately at my high school too."

"What kind of incidents?" A funny, awful feeling was beginning to churn up in my stomach.

"It's nothing too serious, and I don't want you to worry," she said, waving her hand as though brushing away a fly.

It was as if Mama suddenly wanted to take the information back or make it seem less important. But instead of relieving my anxiety, this only made me worry more!

Mama hesitated again before continuing. "A couple of the Jewish students in my class were harassed by older boys. They sound so much like Ivan but stronger and more menacing. One of the Jewish boys ended up with a bloody nose."

"What happened to the bullies?"

"The boys who attacked my students were punished. But I just want you to be extra careful, Dina. Being Jewish is not something to advertise to others these days. Perhaps it's best to stay quiet, keep your head down, and blend a bit into the background. This trouble that's happening lately, hopefully it will all pass soon and things will get back to normal."

I didn't want to blend. I wasn't even sure what that meant! I was proud of my religion and had always been open about it. Both of my parents had taught me to stand up for who I was. But suddenly, Mama was giving me a different message. I glanced over at Papa's picture, wishing for the millionth time that he was here with us.

The grandfather clock chimed nine times. Mama sighed deeply and sat back in her chair.

"My mother is singing to me again," she said wistfully. "So, I think that's enough talk for now. It's time for you to go to bed. I think it's time for all of us to get some sleep," Mama added more loudly, turning to

Nina. But Nina had already finished her cleaning and was standing quite still, looking at us. I realized then that she had heard everything. There was no smile on her face, no dimple that disappeared into a deep crevice. Her face was serious, and even sad.

Long after I had turned out the lights in my room, I thought about that look on Nina's face. Somehow it felt better knowing, or at least imagining, that Nina understood how I felt.

CHAPTER 5

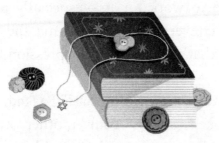

We walked to school the next day in the same formation as the day before—me a few steps ahead of Nina, who was pulling Nadia and pushing the baby carriage. I was lost in my own thoughts, worrying just a bit about whether or not Ivan would be lurking around looking for another fight. A couple of blocks from school, Nina called out to me.

"I need to ask you something, Dina," she said, struggling to catch up to me while pushing the carriage through deep snow. I walked back to her and took over the carriage.

She hesitated, stuttering a bit before getting the question out. "Can you … can you tell me more about being Jewish?"

At first, I was confused. "What do you mean?"

"Explain to me what Jewish is. I knew what your

family's religion was before I came here. But, I've ... I've never worked for a Jewish family before."

I felt a sudden pang of anxiety. Did Nina regret having come to work for us—especially after overhearing my conversation with Mama the night before? Maybe that's what her sad expression had really meant.

"Does Mama know about that?" I asked.

Nina looked away. "Your mother knows I'm Catholic. But she must have thought I had worked for other Jewish families. On my first day, she told me to make sure I didn't mix up the meat and milk dishes. I knew a little bit about that from a friend of mine who once worked for a Jewish family, but I really wasn't sure what it meant."

Nina was referring to the Jewish laws about how we ate certain foods. We couldn't mix meat products with food that contained dairy ingredients. And we had to have separate dishes for those two kinds of meals. It came as second nature to me to know when to use our meat dishes and when to use the dairy plates. But for someone who didn't know about these rules, it would be difficult and confusing to figure it all out.

"I didn't want to tell your mother that I didn't understand it all," Nina continued. "I wanted this job very badly. I liked your mother the moment I met her. I knew yours would be a good family to work for."

"I know Mama won't mind if you explain that this is all new to you," I said.

Nina looked away. "I don't want her to think I deceived her. I'm an honest person. But I just don't know how to bring it up now. That's why I thought you could help me."

I hesitated. Teaching Nina about my religion meant spending more time with her. I was trying to spend as little time with her as possible.

"I've been watching carefully when you set the table," Nina continued. "I'm trying to understand which plates and cutlery you are using for which meal. But it's not just about what you eat. I want to understand more."

Was Nina asking me to explain everything I knew about being Jewish? That would take even more time.

"There's so much I need to learn," Nina continued. "Especially if I'm to continue working for your family." She paused. "And I want to continue."

My anxiety lifted. At least Nina wasn't sorry that she'd come to work for us.

As we rounded the corner and the school came into view, a new plan began bubbling up in my head—something that might be good not only for

Nina but for me as well.

As we neared the gates, I stopped walking. "Okay," I said. "As soon as school is over, we'll go to the library. I'll get some books out for you that talk about Jewish customs and what they mean." I figured I would set Nina up with some books for herself. But this would also give me a chance to be at the library again.

Nina suddenly looked uncertain. "I have to get home after I pick you and your sister up. I need to start the dinner."

She did have a point. Still, if Nina wanted to learn more about my religion, then reading was one of the best ways to do that.

"We'll spend no more than an hour there. You'll still have lots of time to get dinner ready before Mama gets home. I'll help you," I added.

I could see Esther up ahead by the gates, waving at me. I had to go. "I'll see you after school," I said to Nina, and ran off.

The minute school let out, I rushed to find Nina and my sisters. I barely said goodbye to Esther and didn't explain to her what I was doing. Thankfully, there had been no other incidents at school that day.

Nadia held a short branch in her hand as we set

off for the library. "I'm collecting sticks now," she announced. "Maybe I'll build a castle with them when I have enough."

"Nadia, you're going to have to move out of your room soon if you keep bringing things into it," I said. The smile on her face disappeared in an instant.

I sighed. "If you walk quickly to the library now, I'll help you find some sticks on the way home." At that, her face brightened and she picked up her pace.

But today it was Nina who was dragging her feet, stopping often to check on the baby, who was perfectly content in her carriage and not fussing at all.

"Nina," I called back over my shoulder. "We'd better hurry. You're the one who said we needed to get home as quickly as possible." Why was she moving like a snail? At this rate we would have no time at all in the library. "Nina, come on," I called once more, as the library came into view. Finally, almost reluctantly, she caught up with me.

As we entered the building and removed our jackets, my throat caught as memories of Papa flooded over me. The library had been a weekly outing for us, before he got too sick. We had a special routine. First, he let me roam the aisles, picking as many books as I wanted or could carry in my arms. Then we'd sit at one of the many wooden tables that were placed between the stacks. We'd go through each of my chosen books, reading a page or two, talking about the book and what I thought might happen in the story. Finally, he'd let me pick one book, or sometimes two, depending on how long they were. When we got home, Mama would make mint tea with honey. Papa and I would sip our tea together while I dove into my reading.

It was so quiet, I thought as I looked around—the kind of quiet that felt good and peaceful. I breathed in deeply, inhaling the musk of old books. It was a scent I had missed like an old friend.

Looking around for Nina, I saw her standing by the front door, frozen and staring at the high ceiling and rows of shelves sagging under the weight of so many books.

"Come on, Nina," I pleaded again, urging her forward.

First, I sent Nadia off to look for a book on how to build a castle from sticks. I instructed her to search for a book cover that had a castle on it—something she could use as a guide for her construction. I knew that the hunt would keep her busy for a while. The baby was sleeping, thank goodness. We didn't have much time, but at least I could focus.

Nina looked even more uncomfortable than

before. She kept her head down, her arms wrapped around her body as if she were protecting herself. Her eyes, when she finally looked up, darted here and there before settling back down toward the floor.

"Are you feeling okay?" I asked. Nina looked as if she might be getting sick. But when she nodded that she was fine, I pointed to one of the tables. "You can sit here," I said. "I'm going to look for something."

She sank quickly and heavily into one of the chairs as I began to roam the shelves. It didn't take long for me to find the book I wanted. It was a book on Jewish customs that I had seen once before when I'd been here with Papa. I brought the book over to Nina and sat down next to her. Then I opened it, scanned the table of contents, and turned to the section I wanted.

"Here," I said. "You can read this chapter about the Sabbath and how we celebrate every Friday evening and all day Saturday. It's our day of rest." I passed the book over to Nina. She stared at the page and didn't move. "What's the matter?" I asked. "You said you wanted to learn about our customs. Don't you want to do that anymore?"

Nina didn't answer. She continued staring at the page.

"Nina, we don't have much time," I said again, trying hard to keep the frustration out of my voice, but failing miserably. Nina had said that she wanted to learn. But if she had changed her mind or it was no longer that important to her, she should have just said so. Now the minutes were ticking away and I would have no time to look for a book of my own. We would have to rush home to get dinner ready before Mama arrived.

When Nina finally looked up at me, tears were pooled in the corners of her eyes.

"Nina, what's wrong?" I cried.

"I'm … I'm afraid—"

I didn't let her finish. "Afraid of what?"

There was a long moment of silence before Nina finally said, in a voice barely above a whisper, "I'm afraid that I don't know how to read very well."

My mouth dropped open and I stared at Nina, wide-eyed. Not know how to read? How was that possible? Everyone knew how to read. Even Nadia could sound out words in books and she was only six. "Didn't you ever learn in school?"

Nina lowered her eyes again and sighed deeply. "My parents worked on a farm," she explained. "That's where I was raised. There was little opportunity for school and no need for reading." She looked up at me. "I can sign my name, and I understand how to buy things in the market and make change. But other than that ..." Her voice trailed off once more.

"Does Mama know?" I asked.

"Yes, of course." She nodded forcefully. Nina looked down at her hands in her lap. "I've always been unhappy that I was never able to learn."

All the irritation I had been feeling a few minutes earlier disappeared in that moment, evaporated like water into air. Now, I just felt sad for her. And in that moment, another plan suddenly came to me—something that I had to offer Nina, something that might make her feel better.

"Nina, if you want to learn to read, I can teach you."

Without a moment's hesitation, Nina lifted her head. "You would do that?" I nodded, but she still looked uncertain. "Don't you think I'm too old to learn?" she asked.

I stifled a laugh. "No one is too old to learn to read! My papa always said that a person was never too old to learn anything as long as they wanted to. Do you want to learn to read?"

Her eyes suddenly brightened and her wide smile appeared once more. The dimple on the side of her face deepened. "Oh yes. I'd like that very much."

"Okay, then it's a deal. This is the very best place for reading," I said, gesturing around the library.

"We'll come back here as often as we can."

"And I'll make sure that we get home in time for me to get dinner on the table."

I nodded. "We'll start with some simple books. But you'll be reading as well as me in no time at all—maybe even better."

At that Nina laughed out loud. Her eyes were shining. "You're going to teach me to read. I never imagined anything like this could happen!"

I couldn't help but smile. I would be returning to the library often, and that made me very happy. But in that moment, I realized something else: Nina had come into our home to help Mama and my sisters and me. And now I was going to be helpful to her. That realization filled me with more pride and pleasure than I had felt in a long time.

CHAPTER 6

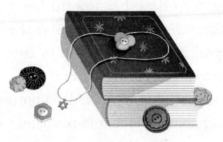

I couldn't wait to tell Mama I was teaching Nina to read. But Nina wouldn't hear of this.

"Who knows if my brain will even be able to learn anything new," she said as we were leaving the library. "I don't want to say I can do something I can't."

"But I know that Mama will be happy to hear that you're trying." Of course Mama would be happy. She was a teacher, after all, eager for people around her to learn new things.

"Please," Nina pleaded. "I want this to be between you and me, for now—just until I see how much I can take in."

We agreed that when the time was right, we would let Mama know. Mama did, however, find out about our excursion to the library. As soon as she walked in the door from work, Nadia ran to tell her about it.

"I found a book about building castles, Mama," Nadia exclaimed. "Come and see it."

"Did you get the book at school?" Mama asked as Nadia began to drag her toward her bedroom. I glanced at Nina. She was standing over the stove, frozen in her spot. It hadn't occurred to either of us to ask Nadia to keep our outing a secret.

"Not at school, Mama," Nadia continued. "We went to the big library. Dina told me where to look."

Mama paused. "You went to the library? All of you?" She turned to look first at me and then at Nina.

"It was my idea," I said quickly. "I hadn't been to the library in such a long time. And Nina agreed to go with us. The baby was quiet and slept the whole time. And we still made it home in plenty of time to get supper ready." I pointed to the table, already set with dishes and cutlery, and to the stove, where Nina had removed the platter of cabbage rolls stuffed with meat and rice from the oven. She turned slowly to face Mama.

"Is it all right with you, Mrs. Sternik? I watched the girls very carefully. I know how important it is to keep them safe." Her voice was soft and a bit shaky.

Nadia was still pulling on Mama's arm. "Come see my book," she pleaded.

Mama paused another second before responding.

"Yes, it's fine—as long as you're careful." She looked at me again. "I suppose I'm being too cautious. After what happened at your school, I thought it would be best to come straight home at the end of the day. But, if you're together, and with Nina, it'll be fine."

"We'll be very careful, Mama. I promise!" Relief flowed through my body. I hadn't lied to Mama about the library—it *had* been my idea. I just hadn't told her everything about why we were going. But she seemed satisfied for now. She even agreed to let us go again whenever we wanted, as long as we watched out for one another. Nina looked just as pleased as I felt.

Now, at the end of each school day, I would rush outside to find Nina and, together with Nadia and the baby, we would head to the library where I sat with her and taught her how to read.

"Why are you in such a hurry?" Esther asked me one afternoon. "I thought you said you didn't need a babysitter."

I couldn't tell her about teaching Nina to read; it wasn't my secret to reveal.

"I don't."

"Then why do you need to run off with her every day? Why don't you come over to my house, like you used to?"

It's true. I'd gotten so caught up in teaching Nina to read that I'd neglected my friendship with Esther. And I did miss spending afternoons with her. If I couldn't tell her the truth, I had to tell her something. "It's just that, with Mama working so much more these days, Nina needs my help at home." I knew that didn't sound convincing, and it wasn't.

Esther's face fell. "Don't you want to do things with me anymore?"

"Of course I do!" I cried. "Look, let's make a plan to meet up on Sunday and go to the park."

Esther's face brightened a bit. "Can we pack a picnic lunch?"

I laughed. "That's a great idea. A winter picnic!"

We gave each other a quick hug, and I headed off to meet up with Nina.

Nina was smart and a fast learner. I started her with the easier books, those with large letters that she could sound out. But it wasn't long before we moved to more complicated stories. I even began teaching her how to write, getting her to copy letters onto a page from the books we chose, and then, as she grew more confident, having her form words on her own. One of the books we read together was about an orphaned girl named Heidi who was living with her grandfather up in the mountains of Switzerland. I had already read the book with Papa when I was first learning to read. It had been a favorite of mine, and I enjoyed reading it again with Nina.

"The grandfather was not very kind at first," Nina said after we'd read several chapters together.

"No," I agreed, "he was kind of grumpy." Because I had read the book, I knew that Heidi would bring her grandfather out of his shell and help him realize all the wonderful things he had in his life. But I didn't tell Nina this, knowing it would give away too much of the story.

A few weeks later, I retrieved the book on Jewish customs that I had found the first time Nina and I came to the library. I set it down in front of her, and we opened it to the section on Passover, the Jewish holiday that observed the freedom of Jewish people from slavery when they were led from Egypt by Moses.

"It reminds me of Easter," she said after reading silently for a few minutes. "They both take place in spring and they're both times to think and pray. In our church we celebrate the Last Supper that our savior had with his disciples. And you have a ..." She searched through the book to find the word. "You have a seder." She looked up at me. "There are so many similarities between our religions." She shook her head and then looked down at her lap, suddenly uncomfortable. "My church teaches us that Jewish people tortured Christian children—even sacrificed a child once during the Easter celebration."

"But that's wrong!" I said, barely able to keep my voice down. "You don't believe that, do you?"

She shook her head. "Of course not! But it was what we learned, and no one questioned it. I didn't even think about it until I came to work for your family." She stared up at me. "Why would my church teach such a horrible thing?"

I sighed, thinking about Ivan and about the students in Mama's school who'd been attacked. I wished I could figure it out myself. But I just couldn't. The baby was starting to get restless, and Nadia was pulling on Nina's arm to take us home.

"Thank you for teaching me," Nina said, before rising.

My heart swelled.

For the first time, Nina signed out two books from the library before leaving. One of them was the book about Jewish customs; the other was the novel about Heidi.

CHAPTER 7

We were in the middle of an early spring thaw—perfect for my winter picnic in the park with Esther. The snow that had filled our backyard was melting, and water fell in fat droplets from the eaves trough of our house.

I had promised Esther that I would be in charge of our lunch. It was the least I could do, after having deserted her on so many afternoons. Though Mama was home, she was busy going over her school material for the following week. So it was Nina who helped me prepare our picnic.

Nina put on her apron and adjusted her head-scarf—deep blue today. I was learning that she had as many scarves as Nadia had sticks in her growing collection. Standing together at the kitchen counter, we sliced bread in thick slabs and piled the slices with

cured meat. Then we wrapped the heaping sandwich-
es in paper and placed them in a small wicker basket along with a small container of pickles, and some
apples that Nina had bought at the market earlier that
week. As I took the basket to the door, she came over
with one more wrapped bundle.

"A special treat for you and Esther," she said with
a smile. I unwrapped a corner of the package to see
a lemon poppy seed cake—another favorite of mine!
I had watched her bake it the day before, thinking it
was for Mama to take to her high school for the other
teachers. I smiled at Nina gratefully and tucked the
cake carefully into the basket. Then I put on my winter coat and pulled my boots up. Mama came over to
me at the door.

"I want you and Esther to be extra careful, Dina,"
she said. She had that same look of worry on her face
that I had seen too many times in the last few weeks.

"It's the park, Mama," I replied. "Esther and I have
been going there together forever."

Mama still looked worried. "I do wish I could
come with you. It's just ..." She looked back at the
table piled with her papers and sighed.

"We'll be fine, Mama. I promise we'll stay
together."

She didn't seem completely convinced. "Maybe

Nina should go with you just to—"

I didn't let her finish. "We'll be fine," I repeated. This was my day with Esther, and I didn't want anything or anyone to interfere with that. I gave Mama a quick kiss on the cheek and grabbed the picnic basket before she could question me further.

"Will you take me too?" Nadia asked before I could bolt out the door. I paused and looked down at my sister.

"Not today, Nadia." Her face fell. "Who will play with the baby if we're both gone?" I asked.

Nadia paused and looked over at Galya, seated on the floor and chewing happily on a wooden block. "Maybe the baby will start to walk today," she said.

"And you can tell me all about it when I get home."

"You stay with me, Nadia," Nina chimed in. "We'll go out for a walk later today. You can look for some lovely sticks for your collection."

"No more sticks," Nadia said. "I think I'm going to start collecting string."

When she turned back to the baby, it gave me the opportunity I needed to finally get out of the house.

Esther was waiting for me at the corner. The sun was shining brightly and we took off down the street, dodging puddles on the sidewalk. Before long, the sweat began to roll down my back, and I opened my jacket and pulled off my wool hat. When I breathed in, I could smell smoke from someone's chimney mixed with the aroma of baking bread and roasted meat. Behind the closed doors on either side of us, I imagined that families were busy preparing their evening's dinner.

"You seem happier with your babysitter these days," Esther said when we slowed to a stroll. She had unbuttoned her red coat, the one I admired so much. Today she wasn't wearing her hat.

"She's nice," I replied.

"Well, I'm glad I don't need a babysitter," Esther continued. Even though Esther's mother helped her father in his tailoring business, she mainly worked from home. That way, she could look after Esther and her young brother.

"I don't need a babysitter either," I said, shifting the picnic basket to my other hand and wiping the sweat from my forehead. "But I like her." It was the first time I had said that, and the words, spoken out loud, resonated deeply within me. It was true, I realized. I did like Nina. I liked that she was so kind to Nadia and the baby. I liked that she was always there to lend a helping hand to Mama. I liked that she didn't try to baby me—she respected the fact that I was older and could be independent. I liked how she had baked a cake for my picnic today. But, perhaps most of all, I liked that I could teach her something. She continued to bring books home from the library and would read them as I helped her prepare supper. We still hadn't said anything to Mama about it. I wasn't sure why. But I believed that it was up to Nina and not me to tell Mama that she was learning to read and write.

"Come on." Esther interrupted my thoughts. "I'll race you to the bridge. Last one there has to clean up the garbage from our picnic."

I shifted the picnic basket one more time and took off after Esther. We ran past our school and past Mrs. Timko's candy store, quiet on this Sunday morning. I was steps behind Esther. I thought she might beat me, and I picked up my pace, passed her, and made it onto the bridge just ahead of her. I stopped in the middle, set the picnic basket down at my feet, and raised my arms above my head.

"Winner!" I declared. "And you weren't even carrying anything."

Esther stopped next to me and bent over, panting to get her breath. "I think you pushed me at the end—made me lose my footing."

I laughed. "Excuses won't get you out of cleaning up after we eat. And I plan to make a big mess." With that, I hoisted the picnic basket once more, and the two of us crossed the bridge and approached the park.

Even from a distance, I could see the park gates, wide open, and a new sign posted above them. It was official looking: a white sign with black stamped letters, and a terrifying image inscribed at the top, the sight of which sent a chill up my spine. It was a swastika, the dreaded symbol of Adolf Hitler's army and his political party. I had seen a couple of these recently—one in the window of a restaurant in town, and another in front of the flower shop that had been owned by Mr. and Mrs. Kaplan. They had provided flowers for every wedding, bar mitzvah, and graduation in town. They had also sent floral arrangements for Papa's funeral and just about every other funeral in the Jewish community. Then one day, that terrible sign was painted on the door to their shop. No one knew who did it. The Kaplans disappeared soon after that. Esther said they were so upset about the vandalism that they left for the countryside where Mrs. Kaplan had a sister. Now the shop was closed and the windows were papered over, though the swastika could still be seen on the door, faded but visible. I avoided going by the shop. The sign reminded me that a Jewish family had been driven away.

Esther and I approached the park gate and came

to a dead stop in front of it, staring at the symbol. My heart began to race and my legs felt shaky. The letters below the swastika were blurry at first. I blinked several times. It took another couple of seconds before the writing came into focus. The message was short and clear.

Jews are no longer permitted to enter the park.
Any Jew caught inside will be arrested.
By order of the mayor and the city council.

"Why?" Esther whispered after we had stood in silence for another minute.

I shook my head. "I don't know."

"What should we do?"

I didn't know the answer to that either.

"Should we leave?" Esther asked.

"Maybe we should ignore it and just go inside anyway," I replied defiantly. Who was going to stop two young girls from playing in the park? We weren't doing anything to hurt anyone. We just wanted to have a picnic. The basket that I still held in my hand suddenly felt so heavy.

"But what if someone sees us?" Esther said. She pointed at the sign. "It says we could get arrested. I don't think we should go in."

"But this is so wrong!"

I looked over at Esther. Her eyes had grown as round as two moons and a new line of sweat had beaded up across her forehead. I knew that this time it wasn't because of the spring thaw and the warmth of the sun that still shone brightly above us. Esther was sweating out of fear. And I felt the same way. I may have sounded as if I was willing to defy the order on the sign, but in my heart, I knew Esther was probably right. Maybe I could stand up to a bully like Ivan, but it was far more dangerous to fight the city council, or the government that didn't want Jews to be part of the community. I was crazy to think we could.

On the other side of the open gate, just steps away from us, I could see a group of children running across the park field. A couple of kids were climbing a tall tree. Two boys had flung their jackets off to one side and were kicking a soccer ball back and forth. The pond in the far corner still had a thin layer of ice. But that didn't stop a young boy and girl from skipping stones across it. I wasn't any different from those children, I thought. I had played next to them in this same park since I was Nadia's age, or younger. But my religion was suddenly keeping us far apart, separating us just like this iron gate. The freedom and fun on the other side now seemed so far away. A young mother sat on a park bench under a tree, pushing a baby carriage back and forth to soothe her crying baby.

I wanted to cry too. I wanted to scream that this was unfair and unjust. But I knew that it would do no good.

"Do you want to go somewhere else for our picnic?" Esther asked halfheartedly.

I shook my head. "I don't think so. I'm kind of tired."

Esther nodded. "I guess I am too."

We stared at the sign a while longer. I don't know what we were waiting for or what we expected might happen. Maybe we thought if we stared long enough, the letters on the sign would fade and disappear, and we would be invited back inside.

Finally, without saying another word, I picked up the picnic basket. Linking arms with Esther, we slowly and silently walked away.

CHAPTER 8

When we were nearly home, Esther and I stopped and turned to one another.

"I'll see you at school tomorrow?" she asked.

I could tell she was hoping I would reassure her that everything would be fine when we saw each other the next day. I nodded. "Let's not worry too much about this," I replied.

"Oh, I won't," she said.

We exchanged a quick hug and parted ways. I don't think either of us believed the other.

The minute I walked in the door, I blurted the whole story out to Mama in one long gulp. I hardly took a breath as I described the sign on the gate at the entrance to the park and the swastika that had stood out like a tall, ugly weed in the middle of a field of flowers. All the while I was talking, Nina hovered in the background, listening but saying nothing. I didn't mind that she heard me. I had come to realize that I could trust her. I wanted her to know what was happening. Thank goodness Nadia was in her room. I didn't want to scare her with my story. Even the baby was sitting tall in her high chair, her eyes fixed on me as if she knew something was wrong.

When I finished talking, I was exhausted, breathing hard, as if I had just run a race. I waited for my mother to say something. What I really wanted was for her to tell me that it was nothing—a temporary mistake that would be fixed soon and Esther and I would be able to go back to playing in the park as we had always done. I wanted her to tell me that nothing more would happen, that nothing *bad* would happen. I wanted Mama to reassure me that everything was okay, just as Esther had wanted that same reassurance from me.

But that's not what happened. There was a look on Mama's face that I hadn't seen since Papa had died. Fear. It was blooming in her eyes like a wildflower in the mountains. Her mouth sagged, her cheeks grew pale, and her eyes darted first to me and then to Nina.

"Mama?" My mouth had become dry and words felt as if they were sticking in my throat.

Mama swallowed hard. "I can't believe it's happening," she finally whispered.

"What? What's happening?"

"The trouble in other countries. I can't believe it's all coming here."

This wasn't what I wanted to hear. There was a war going on in those other countries: Germany, Poland, Austria, and more. Was Mama suggesting that the war was moving here?

"This isn't as bad as other places, is it, Mama?" I asked, half afraid to hear the answer. "Those terrible things that are happening to Jewish people in other countries—they're not going to happen here, are they?" Mama had talked about Jewish people being arrested just for being Jewish. She had even hinted at prisons that were being built far away from the big cities where Jewish men, women, and even children were being sent. They were being tortured and even killed in those prisons. It was one thing to know that some Jewish students in my town had been beaten up, or that bullies like Ivan were flexing their muscles. It was another thing to think that all the Jews of my country might be in danger. And yet, that sign in the park sent a clear message that we weren't wanted.

I glanced over at the portrait of Papa hanging on the wall. His gaze was so calm and strong. I wanted to draw strength from it. But his picture and the memory of his strength would do us little good if we were really threatened. I suddenly felt even more afraid.

"Should we leave?" I whispered. I was thinking about the Kaplans and their flower shop.

"I can't imagine where we'd go—me, a single mother with three children," Mama replied. Then she glanced at me and shook her head slightly from side to side, as if she were coming out of a fog and realizing what her words must have sounded like—how terrifying her message was.

"I'm so sorry, my darling," she said. "I forget sometimes that you're still young. You understand more than you should."

For once, I wished I didn't understand so much. I wished I seemed as innocent and naive as Nadia or the baby.

"What are we going to do?" I asked.

Mama squared her shoulders and breathed in deeply. "What we are going to do is keep our heads down and avoid any trouble."

Would keeping my head down protect me? I wasn't sure.

"I told you before that you shouldn't draw too much attention to yourself as a Jewish girl," Mama continued. "And that's more important than ever. You'll go to school as always. Come home right after." She turned to Nina. "I don't want the children on the streets for long periods of time. Bring them home straight after school ends."

Nina nodded. "Yes, Mrs. Sternik. I'll make sure they're safe."

Mama looked satisfied. "Good. We'll obey whatever laws come out. That's something we have to do. But hopefully, all this will pass and everything will go back to normal soon."

I stared at Mama. For the first time in my life, I didn't believe her.

CHAPTER 9

Mama wouldn't allow us to go to the library anymore, which was probably the worst kind of punishment for me. The library had always been my safe haven. But a few days after the park incident, Mama said that a Jewish boy had been harassed by some thugs in front of the library building, and my safe haven suddenly didn't feel so safe. Nina offered to go on her own in her spare time and bring me books that she thought I might like to read. She always added a book for herself.

Now, when we walked to school, I no longer ran ahead of her, pretending I wasn't with her. I stayed by her side. I was still afraid of all the things that Mama had talked about. Staying next to Nina felt safer. And as we walked, Nina talked about the book she was reading, what she liked and didn't like about it, and

what she was hoping to read next. Those conversations helped distract me.

The spring thaw that had started a couple of
weeks ago had lasted. We had not had another snow-
fall and the temperatures continued to climb. Early
spring flowers were already pushing out of the bare
flowerbeds on either side of Mrs. Timko's store as we
walked past. I had abandoned my winter coat in favor
of a lighter jacket. Mrs. Timko had only a thin shawl
wrapped around her shoulders. I said good morning
and reached into her basket for my usual treat. Nina
paused to greet Mrs. Timko and chat with her. Esther
was there that morning as well. She pulled me aside
after claiming a candy for herself.

"Did you ever talk to your mother about what
happened in the park?" she asked. It was the first time
we had spoken about the incident. In the intervening
weeks we had avoided the topic, almost pretending it
hadn't happened. I was surprised to hear Esther ask
about it today.

I nodded. "Did you tell your parents?"

"I told them everything," Esther said.

"What did they say?"

"They didn't seem as worried as I'd thought they'd
be. They said they hoped the sign would be gone soon
and we'd be able to go back there."

I frowned. "My mother wasn't so sure of that. She said she hoped things would go back to normal. But I think she's more scared than your parents seem to be."

I wanted to believe Esther's parents, to believe that everything would be fine. But that look of fear on Mama's face still haunted me.

"I'll be at the gate waiting for you at the end of the day," Nina said as the school bell rang up ahead.

I entered my classroom with Esther. Mr. Petrenko was standing at the door, greeting us as we walked in. I nodded politely and took my seat. Ever since the incident with Ivan and Avrum, I hadn't had much interaction with my teacher. I answered questions in class and did my homework, but I no longer volunteered for extra assignments as I had done in the past. I guess I was keeping my head down, as Mama would say.

Mr. Petrenko limped to the front of the class and faced us. But instead of asking us to open our books, he asked us all to stand up.

Along with everyone else, I shuffled my chair back and stood next to my desk. I exchanged a glance with Esther, but she looked just as confused as I was.

"There's going to be a … a slight change in the seating plan starting today," Mr. Petrenko said.

Why did my teacher look so nervous? He was running his hand through his hair, and clasping and unclasping his fingers. I could see a line of sweat down the side of his face. It was warm in the classroom, but not that warm.

Mr. Petrenko began calling students' names and moving them to different seats. Occasionally in the past, students had been moved to other desks. One boy, Stephan, had been moved to the front when he lost his glasses. He had said it would be weeks before his family could get him another pair. Mr. Petrenko had moved him up where he could see the blackboard. And another girl, Blanka, had been moved to the front when she hurt her ankle. The front of the room was closer to the door, and Blanka could more easily walk in and out without tripping over all the other desks.

But this reorganization was different. Mr. Petrenko began to move groups of students, not just one or two. Some went to the front and others were sent to the back. There didn't seem to be any logic to this complete reorganization of the classroom. And then, he said my name.

"Eldina Sternik, please take your books and move to a seat at the back of the room," Mr. Petrenko said.

My heart sank. I loved my seat in the second row.

It was the perfect spot. It was close enough that I could hear everything Mr. Petrenko was saying and I could see everything he wrote on the blackboard. At the same time, I was protected by one student in front of me. That was especially important when I didn't know the answer to a question and Mr. Petrenko was searching the room for someone to target. I could slouch down and hide so that he wouldn't pick me. I didn't like the idea of being in the last row. But it seemed I had no choice.

Slowly and reluctantly, I gathered my books and headed for the back. I slumped into an empty seat in the last row and looked around. The blackboard seemed very far away. Everything seemed far away. The only consolation was that Esther was in a desk beside me. In the past, Mr. Petrenko had separated us so that we wouldn't be tempted to chat with one another. I gave her a weak grin and gazed again to the left and to the right. That was when the realization of what had happened began to sink in. And when it did, my stomach plunged and my spirits with it.

All the students who had been moved to the back of the classroom were Jewish: me, Esther, Avrum, another girl, Dora, a boy, Bruno, along with all the others. We had all been set apart from the rest of the class and moved to the back like day-old pastries in the bakery shop. It was just like being back in the park and seeing the sign that had forbidden Jewish people from entering. It didn't matter that we were all young Ukrainian boys and girls—proud of our country. The only thing that seemed to matter was our religion, and mine was the wrong one to have—at least that's what it felt like.

Just then, Ivan, who had been seated several rows ahead of us, turned and stared at me. Sneering, he quietly mouthed the words, "Stinky Jew!" Several other students sitting close to him laughed.

My face burned and I sank even lower into my seat, soaking in the cruel taunt and feeling even more rejected. Mr. Petrenko limped down the aisle a few seconds later. His lame leg, as he swung it around, banged noisily into one of the desks. He stumbled, and struggled to regain his footing. I looked up at him. He glanced into my eyes and then quickly turned away. He didn't look at me again for the rest of the day.

CHAPTER 10

So much had changed so quickly. At school, I sat in the back row and didn't say much anymore. Esther and I no longer saw each other outside of school hours. There were no more outings, and no other opportunities to meet up with her. Mama didn't want me going over to her house after school. And even though Esther's parents hadn't seemed as concerned about the sign on the park gate, they also didn't want Esther out on the streets except to go to school and back home. I played in the yard with my sisters and helped Nina with the chores. But gradually, the house felt as if it was closing in on me. The ceiling felt lower, and the walls a bit closer. I felt at times like a prisoner. I wasn't being kept behind bars, but I may as well have been, for all the freedom that I had lost.

I worried more about Mama. Esther had told me

that some Jewish people her father knew had lost their jobs when their employers no longer wanted them in their businesses. She said that many people had stopped ordering suits from her father. Few Jewish men could afford a suit when they had less and less money to put food on the table for their families. Food was more important than clothing, she said. And of course, that was true. Mama hadn't lost her job, but I was scared that she might. And I worried for her safety. Every evening, I stood by the window watching for her. And I felt a huge wave of relief when I saw her round the corner and approach the front door of our home. Each day that passed with no incidents felt like a victory. I never asked her if things were going to get back to normal. I didn't have to. Nothing was normal. We were okay as long as things didn't get worse.

The days were starting to get longer. So instead of arriving home in the dark, Mama would appear in the soft glow of twilight. One evening, as I stood watching her approach, I could see something different and troubling. She looked tired, but that wasn't unusual. Mama always looked tired at the end of the day. It was the way she was walking that worried me. Her shoulders were drooping forward and her feet were dragging as if she had climbed a steep hill or sprinted a long distance. I gulped when I saw her, and my stomach clenched.

Just before entering the house, she paused, drew back her shoulders, and raised her chin. But as soon as she walked in the door, I could see the dark circles under her eyes and the pastiness of her skin. I helped her out of her jacket. But instead of grabbing me and my sisters into her usual hug, she dropped into a chair at the table and closed her eyes.

"Mama! Are you okay? Are you not feeling well?" I was growing more and more alarmed by her looks and by the way her body sagged.

It took a couple of seconds before Mama straightened up and opened her eyes.

"Dina, come sit next to me," she said, patting the chair by her side. "Nadia, you come over here too. And Nina," she addressed our housekeeper, "I need you to hear this as well."

Nadia walked over to Mama. Nina stopped stirring the big pot of soup that had been bubbling on the stove. She wiped her hands on her apron and walked toward us. When we had all assembled in front of her, my mother reached into her bag and pulled out several large panels of yellow fabric. When I looked closely at them, I could see that they had been stamped with the black outline of dozens of small Stars of David.

How strange, I thought. The Star of David was an important symbol of our religion. There was a big one on top of the synagogue, and another one atop the beautiful menorah that we lit every year on Chanukah, the festival of lights. And there was one engraved into the headstone in the cemetery where Papa was buried. But these sheets of yellow fabric with perfectly aligned Stars of David made no sense to me.

"What's that for?" Nadia asked. She picked up a panel of fabric and drew her finger around the outline of one of the stars.

Mama sighed heavily. "It's another rule that came out today. Every Jewish citizen must wear these stars on their clothing—one sewn on the front and one on the back of every sweater, blouse, and jacket that we own."

At first, I didn't understand. "But why?"

Mama shook her head. "I'm trying to understand it myself. I think it's just another way to identify us— let everyone know that we're Jewish."

A cold chill descended over me. It was one thing to close the park to Jewish citizens, or move me and my Jewish friends to the back of the classroom. Mama had told me to keep my head down, which I was trying to do. But now, we had to wear our religion on our clothing, marking us for everyone to see. It would be impossible to avoid being identified as Jewish if we wore this symbol on all our clothes.

"Can we refuse to do it?" I whispered. It was the same question I'd asked Esther when we had stood together outside the park.

Mama shook her head. "No."

"Why not?"

"Jews will be arrested if they refuse to wear the star."

"But who will know?" I persisted.

The dark circles around Mama's eyes seemed to grow even darker. "People will know. Our neighbors know we're Jewish. The vendors in the market, the people at the bank, the police in town—everyone knows our religion. We've never hidden it. People are being encouraged to identify Jews to the authorities, especially those who are not wearing their stars. We can't take that risk."

"I love the star," Nadia said. "It's pretty."

Mama reached up and stroked Nadia's cheek. "That's good, my darling, because we'll cut out all these lovely stars and sew them on all your blouses. Will you help me with that?"

Nadia nodded. Then Mama looked back at me. "We're better off following the rules. And hopefully, this will be the last one!"

That's what Mama had said when the sign in the park appeared. I didn't remind her of that.

Nina stepped forward. "I'll help with the sewing," she said. "But first, you all need to have a good supper."

No one spoke as we ate. Nadia swung her legs back and forth under her. The persistent squeak of her chair was the sound that accompanied our silence— that, and our grandfather clock that ticked away in the background. After I had helped Nina clear away the dishes, we set the yellow sheets of cloth on the table and Nina and I began to cut the stars out, carefully following the straight black lines. Even Nadia helped with a few of them, working more diligently than I had ever seen, tracking the outline of each star. Watching her take the scissors in her small hands and slice through the fabric made my chest ache and only worsened the fear that was already consuming me. I was terrified! And fear wasn't something you could turn off like I turned my reading lamp off every night. Quietly, I began to bring all of our clothing to the table. The pile of dresses, blouses, sweaters, and jackets grew until there was a mountain of garments piled high in the kitchen.

We worked for hours, stitching the stars onto the

front and back of every single outfit we owned. We worked to the beat of our grandfather clock. Mama had said that the ticking was like her mother's heartbeat. I wondered what my grandmother would have thought about us having to wear these stars. My face burned as we worked. I thought about what Nadia had said earlier, and so innocently. She had said that she loved the stars. Well, I loved the Star of David too. I had always felt proud of it. But in that moment, as we labored over the sewing, I felt nothing but shame.

It was late before we all finally went to bed. I was just about to turn off my reading lamp when Nina came into my bedroom. In her hand she carried one of my sweaters. I could see the star on the front of it as she sat down on the edge of my bed. She stared deeply into my eyes.

"I don't really want to talk, Nina," I said.

"I understand, but I'd like you to hear this." She held the sweater out in front of her. "This doesn't change who you are inside. You must always remain proud of that."

I couldn't answer, blinking back tears. Nina understood how horrible all these rules were—how unbearable it was to be singled out like this. She had been open to learning about my religion. I had to believe that if Nina understood that we were human beings, no better or worse than anyone else, then others had to understand it as well. At least that's what I hoped.

CHAPTER 11

No matter what Nina had said about being proud of who I was, I dreaded my walk to school the next day. I kept my eyes fixed on the sidewalk, but just couldn't shake the feeling that everyone on the street was staring at me, and that the stars sewn onto my coat were the only thing anyone would see. Were people pointing at me? Were they whispering behind my back? I couldn't bear to look up to find out.

Nadia appeared oblivious to the stars that seemed to glow off her chest and her back. She walked beside Nina, showing her a long red thread she held tight in her hand. She had moved on to collecting pieces of thread and string, just as she had said she would. She took a lot of them from Mama's sewing kit.

I wished I could be as innocent and carefree as my younger sister. I wished I could go back in time and be a child like her, or a baby like Galya, cooling in her carriage. But that was as impossible as changing the law that had ordered us to wear these stars.

I glanced up only when we passed the candy store. Mrs. Timko was in her usual spot, smiling and calling out to the children to take a sweet. That, at least, would help brighten this day. I looked around for Esther, but she was nowhere to be seen. I knew that she too would be wearing a star on her beautiful red jacket. What did her parents think about that? I wondered. Did they still think everything would be fine? Did they think this rule, like the sign in the park, would disappear?

Nina smiled and waved at Mrs. Timko. But when she realized how big the line was in front of the candy store, her face fell. "We don't have too much time today, Dina," Nina said. "It's late, and school will be starting soon."

"It'll just take a minute or two, Nina. Please," I added. There was no way I was going to miss out on a treat today.

"You wait with Nina," I said to Nadia. "I'll get you a candy. I'll be quick."

My sister seemed content with that, and I joined the crowd of children inching closer to Mrs. Timko. I didn't see any other kids with stars on their clothing in the crowd. And so far, no one seemed to have noticed me. Slowly but surely, I moved forward, waiting patiently for my turn to claim a candy. There was just one boy in front of me now. Mrs. Timko passed the basket to him. When he stepped aside, I moved up and Mrs. Timko caught sight of me. Her eyes moved from mine to the front of my blouse, and the star. She paused, and then, for the first time I could ever remember, the smile disappeared from her face. Her eyes narrowed, her brow creased, and she sucked in her breath.

"No candy for you!" she said.

My hand froze midway to the basket. I looked up at Mrs. Timko. Had I heard her correctly? It wasn't possible!

"I beg your pardon?" I asked.

She pulled the basket back toward her and wrinkled her nose. "I said no candy for the JEWISH girl." That's how it sounded to my ears—like she had put my religion in capital letters and shouted it loudly so that everyone around her could hear.

The other children who had gathered for their daily treat turned to stare at me, my hand still outstretched toward the basket that had been pulled away. This was my nightmare come alive. My face burned like the coals that glowed in the fireplace on a winter's night. Suddenly, Nina was beside me.

"There's no need for that," she said in a low and steady voice. But I could feel her hand trembling as she placed it on my shoulder, whether in fear or anger, I couldn't tell.

"They're nothing but trouble," Mrs. Timko continued, facing Nina. "You should know that. The Jews will take over our business and schools if we let them."

"She's only a child," Nina said, tightening her grip on my shoulder.

Mrs. Timko looked hard at her. "A Jewish child."

Nina would not back down. "A CHILD, just like the others." Her other hand swept over the crowd. And then she turned back to Mrs. Timko. "You should be ashamed of yourself!" She spit the words out.

Mrs. Timko pressed her lips together. "Best you don't help that family anymore," she said to Nina. "Or people like them. You could get into trouble too."

Nina pulled herself up, trying to make herself look taller than her tiny frame. When she spoke, her voice was still quiet. But every word cut like a knife. "I will help ANYONE. I. CHOOSE!"

The children all around me were still staring. Several pointed at my star, and still others backed away from me as if I was a dangerous animal or I had a disease they might catch. These were some of the same children from my class who had snickered when I'd been moved to the back with the other Jewish children. I wanted to disappear into the pavement.

Nina put her arm firmly around my shoulders. "Let's go," she said. I looked at her. If she was shaken by the incident, she wasn't showing it.

Nadia had come up behind us. She reached up to take my hand. "Do I get a candy today, Dina?" she asked.

"Not today, Nadia," I said, grasping her hand tightly and pulling her close to me. "Maybe another day."

Nina glared back at Mrs. Timko one more time. Then we turned and walked away.

CHAPTER 12

Jews couldn't go to the movie theater.

Jews couldn't shop in any stores.

Jews had to be off the street at a certain time.

It seemed that every day more and more rules were passed limiting our freedom. We learned about some of the rules on the radio, and others from the newspaper that Mama brought home most nights.

We even had to hand my bicycle over to the authorities. The truth is, since Papa's death, I had hardly ridden my bike. The chain was rusted and had come off the rail. But still, this law nearly drove me crazy. What danger was a bicycle?

Perhaps the most painful rule was that the library was closed to Jews. We hadn't been in a long time, but it still broke my heart to know that the place I had loved to go was formally off limits.

With each new law, I would look to Mama for her reaction. Her body seemed to be shrinking right in front of my eyes. Her shoulders were always hunched now, as if the weight of these rules was too much for her. Her breathing was sometimes quick and shallow. Her voice lost its lightness. Her hair was dull. I didn't have to ask her if she was worried. I could see it.

And then one day, Mama came home to announce that she was no longer permitted to work. Her high school had let her and all the other Jewish teachers go. I had been dreading this news, but I couldn't say I was surprised.

"Well, at least I'll have more time to be with you and your sisters," Mama said, bravely trying to smile through the tears that were gathering in the corners of her eyes. She turned to Nina. "With me at home, I'm not sure we really need a housekeeper anymore. And money will be tight. I have some savings that I've put aside. But I'm afraid there won't be much left over to pay you, Nina."

Nina took a long breath in. "I was worried that this might happen, Mrs. Sternik—you losing your job. I'm so sorry it has to be this way."

"But this isn't your fault."

"No, but I feel ashamed that Jewish people are being treated like this. It's not right."

"I wish more people thought the way you do," Mama whispered.

"I know what's right and wrong," Nina replied. "No matter what laws are passed."

Mama shook her head. "As I said, I won't have much to pay you with, Nina. I'll understand if you need to leave us."

Nina's eyes widened. "But I couldn't imagine leaving," she exclaimed. "I care for all of you so much." She scanned the room, letting her eyes rest on Nadia, the baby, and then on me. "You're like my family now."

"But what if you're no longer allowed to work for a Jewish family?" I asked.

Nina shook her head. "I'll figure that out when and if I have to." She looked back at Mama. "In the meantime, if you want me, I'll stay."

I nearly shouted *yes* out loud. We had lost so much, and I couldn't bear the thought of losing Nina too. But I didn't have to say a word.

"And you're our family as well," Mama said, her voice breaking. "I don't know what any of us would do without you." The tears were flowing down Mama's cheeks, but she looked as happy as I was to hear that Nina was staying.

I walked over and wrapped my arms around

Nina's small, solid body, realizing that this was the first time I'd ever hugged her. Nina's arms crept up my back, patting me gently in return. It felt good to be in her arms: good and safe. A second later, I felt someone tug on my sweater. It was my little sister.

"I want to hug too," Nadia said. I smiled and Nina pulled Nadia into the circle. I wasn't sure whether or not my sister understood what was happening. But I knew how much she loved Nina and how much she wanted to show it.

We stood like that until Mama came over. She took Nina's hands and squeezed them hard. "Are you sure about this, Nina?" Mama asked. "It's a big decision to make."

"I'm sure," Nina replied. "I'm staying, no matter what." She sniffled, bringing her apron up to her eyes and dabbing at them. Then she turned back to the stove and to the stew that was threatening to boil over. The lid was rattling off the pot. "That's enough of that," she said. "Look what you've all done. You've made me very nearly burn our supper. Food is what we all need right now."

Later that night, I was still awake long after the others had gone to sleep. My mind kept turning over the events of the last few months and the realization that everything was going from bad to worse. Just a few months ago, my biggest worry had been whether or not I would get a good grade in school. I used to care only about how often I'd get to see Esther, or whether or not Mama was going to take me shopping, or if I'd have to babysit Nadia instead of going outside to play. The memories began almost like a fairy tale: Once upon a time I had … Once I saw … Once I thought … But there was no *happily ever after* to my imaginings. Now I worried about whether there would be enough food to eat, or whether someone was going to bully me. How had everything gone so bad in such a short time? And what horrible thing would happen next? None of it made sense. Finally, I sat up and turned my light back on, pushing my hands up against the sides of my head to try to stop all those thoughts from invading my brain. But I couldn't get rid of them. I knew it did no good to dream about what had been. That only made you crazy. It wasn't as if I could turn back time or return to a better place. And it did no good to worry about what was coming. That could make you crazy as well.

There was a soft knock at my bedroom door. "Come in," I said.

I thought it might be Mama reminding me I had school the next day and telling me to turn off the lights and go to sleep. But it was Nina's head that peeked in the doorway.

"Can I come in?"

I nodded and she entered. She was wearing a nightgown and housecoat cinched at the waist with a long rope. Her hair, even for bedtime, was covered with a scarf—this time deep green.

"Can't you sleep?" she asked as she came over to stand above my bed.

"No. I keep thinking about everything that's happening. Why, Nina? Why are people so hurtful? And why are Jewish people the ones everyone hates? What's wrong with us?" The questions poured out of me in one long stream.

"Nothing is wrong with you!" Nina answered forcefully. "Nothing at all. You mustn't ever think that."

"It's so hard not to." How could I not become discouraged when everyone was telling us that we were bad and worthless?

Nina sat heavily on the edge of my bed. "I was ignorant about your faith at one time, do you remember? But you and your family have taught me so much. People are afraid of what they don't know. I wish they could learn to understand more."

I wished that too. But all the understanding in the

world wasn't going to stop those laws from happening. I was sure about that.

"I thought that Mrs. Timko was a good person—a kind person," Nina continued. "I was wrong. Too many are just like her."

We hadn't gone past the candy store in so long—taking a longer route to school that avoided Mrs. Timko.

Nina sighed. "Sometimes, I think your family should run far away from here, or go to stay with someone who might protect you."

Mama had said that it was impossible for our family to get away. And as for going to someone who could help us, I knew there wasn't really anyone. Papa had a brother who lived somewhere in town. We never saw him, and I barely remembered him. He had married a Christian woman and that pretty much ended his relationship with the family. I didn't understand too much about it. All I knew was that he had disappeared from our lives.

We sat in silence for a few more seconds. And then I asked, "You're not going to leave us, are you?" Nina had told Mama that she would stay, no matter what. But I also needed to hear her say that to me. She reached over to take my hand.

"I won't leave. I promise you."

I could feel tears gathering behind my eyes, and I blinked furiously.

"Besides," Nina added, a smile threatening to take over her face. "Who will read and write with me if I leave you?"

I smiled sadly, knowing full well that Nina no longer needed me to help her with her reading and writing. She could do that on her own. But still I worried. "Don't you have someone—someone who wants you to come home to them?" I knew Nina wasn't married; Mama had told me that even before Nina had come to stay with us. But might there be some pull from somewhere for her to leave? I knew she came from the country, and I knew she had been a housekeeper for many years. But I had never asked this question of her before.

"No," she replied. And then she suddenly seemed to grow shy. She looked away. "There once was a boy," she finally said. "It was so many years ago."

I look at her. "Someone that you were in love with?"

"Yes. He came to my father to ask permission to marry me. But he was poorer than we were. 'How will he support you?' my father asked. 'And what dowry can he possibly give?' In the end, my father said no to him. No one came after that." Nina closed her eyes.

I watched her, wondering if she was remembering the boy who loved her and whom she had once loved. "But you never had any children," I said. "Aren't you sad about that?"

Nina's eyes opened quickly and widened. "But I have you! And I have Nadia and the baby. And there are so many other children that I've cared for over the years. I've loved you all as if you were my own."

I lowered my eyes at that, realizing for a moment that Nadia, Galya, and I weren't the only children Nina had looked after. "Did you love any of the other children more than me?" I felt embarrassed to ask the question, but it was out of my mouth before I could stop myself.

Nina smiled that giant smile that I hadn't seen in some time. It stretched across her face, and the dimple in her cheek deepened. "How could I love any of them more than you? I think you must be my favorite of all time." She leaned even closer to me. "But perhaps that should be our secret."

In my heart I knew she had probably shared that same secret with lots of other children. I could still pretend I was the only one.

"Now, do you think you could try to get some sleep?" she asked, rising from my bed. "At this rate, the sun will be up before you've even closed your eyes. And you'll be stumbling into school tomorrow."

I nodded. Nina said goodnight and left the room. I rolled over and closed my eyes. The last thought I had before I finally fell asleep was a realization that while everything had changed for the worse in these last months, one thing was better. I had Nina in my life. I had gone from being suspicious of her to loving her and needing her more than I ever imagined I would.

CHAPTER 13

It came as no surprise to me when, one week later, I arrived at school to find another big sign posted on the building.

Nadia had woken with a fever. Mama was also sick with a raging headache. She could barely lift her head from the bed and needed to stay put in a darkened room where it was quiet. So, rather than walk me to school as usual, Nina had to stay home with the baby to tend to Mama and Nadia. I tiptoed into Mama's room to tell her that I was going to go over to Esther's house early so that she and I could walk to school together. Even though I could walk to school on my own, I no longer felt entirely safe doing so.

"We'll be extra careful," I said, keeping my voice low as I hovered over Mama's bed. She opened her eyes and tried to focus on me. But she didn't say a word. "We'll go straight to school and then come straight home," I continued.

I waited for Mama to grill me about how to stay safe. I waited for her to make me promise to stay away from any trouble, to stay close to Esther, and of course to keep my head down. But today, she seemed to have no strength to do anything but nod reluctantly and then close her eyes again.

Instead, it was Nina who walked me through the safety rules, asking me to repeat them until she was satisfied that I would stay out of harm's way, or know what to do if there was any trouble. She was watching out for me, just like Mama. Nina's voice was even beginning to sound like Mama's, I thought with a start—the same words, the same firm tone in her warnings.

Spring was definitely in the air as Esther and I walked to school. It had rained the night before and clusters of mushrooms had sprouted up at the side of the road. But the early morning sun poked through the tree branches that were expanding nearly in front of our eyes as leaves pushed out of their buds. Birds flew lazily overhead. It was going to be another warm day.

Esther was still wearing her beautiful red coat, now unbuttoned and pulled slightly off her shoulders.

By now, her father should have made her a new spring jacket. But she'd told me that he was struggling to find work. With no money, there would be no new clothing for Esther this spring. My spring jacket had grown too small for me. It pulled across my chest, and my arms jutted from the sleeves like two stalks of celery. The jacket was destined to become Nadia's and probably should have been hers already. But for now, I had nothing to replace it. As we approached the school, I was about to pull the jacket off my shoulders and let it hang behind me when I spied a large new sign beside the doors. Esther came to a dead stop, and I had to pull her along to the front of the school building, where we stared up at the black lettering and tried to make sense of the wording. I didn't even notice Ivan until he had come up next to me.

"What are you doing here?" he asked, moving in front of us. "Didn't you see this?" He pointed behind him to the sign. "It says, 'Jews are forbidden to attend school. This building is closed to Jews.'" He turned to face us once more. "There, I've read it for you."

"I'm impressed," I said, almost without thinking. "Your reading skills have improved."

"Dina," Esther whispered, reaching out to grab my arm. Then she turned to Ivan. "She didn't mean that."

"Yes, I did," I snapped.

Ivan pulled himself up and inhaled sharply. "You don't belong here. It's *our* school now." He took a step toward us. "Go away!"

For a moment, neither Esther nor I moved. We stood facing Ivan. I wanted to say something more. I wanted to shout at him and tell him to step aside. In the past, he would have backed down if I confronted him. But everything had changed. The law was now on Ivan's side. He and others could order me to wear a star on my clothing, stay out of the park, or stop going to school, and I had to do it. Esther was still pulling on my arm, and her eyes pleaded with me to leave the schoolyard. Finally, I turned away.

"Don't run," I whispered to her as we walked away from the building. "I don't want to give Ivan the satisfaction of thinking we're scared."

But of course, I was scared! I may have sounded fierce, but inside I was quaking. And I knew Esther was as well. It was only when we were out of the schoolyard that we picked up our pace. We ran past the synagogue, the library, and the market. We didn't stop running until we had parted ways and I arrived at home, bursting through the doors.

Mama was sitting in the kitchen along with Nadia, Nina, and the baby. Nadia's cheeks still burned bright red, and Mama still looked unwell. One elbow rested on the table under her chin. It looked as if her head would fall over if she didn't hold it up. Her cheeks were pale and her lips were drawn in. My heart was still pounding, and my head was buzzing. I wanted so badly to tell everything that had happened, but something stopped me. The radio, which usually sat in a corner of the sitting room, had been moved to the middle of the kitchen table. My family was gathered around it, listening intently to a news report that echoed through the room. No one, not even the baby, seemed to notice me. No one registered that I was home from school almost before the day had started. I paused at the doorway and listened.

"*The army of the Third Reich under the leadership of Adolf Hitler continues to move into Ukraine and conquer all of the territories.*"

The announcer began to list the cities in my country that were already under the control of Adolf Hitler.

"Polonne, Letichev, Felshtin ..."

On and on he went while I waited, holding my breath and hoping that I wouldn't hear the name of my city. But a moment later, all my hopes were shattered.

"And Proskurov," the announcer said.

Mama sucked in her breath and finally raised her

head to look at me. "Dina, how long have you been standing there?"

"I heard it all, Mama," I cried. "Proskurov has been invaded by the Nazis?"

"Yes," she whispered.

I told Mama about what had happened at school. I didn't think it was possible for her cheeks to grow any paler. But as I spoke, her face became completely ashen.

"There's no school?" Nadia asked, looking from me to Mama.

Mama answered Nadia for me. "No, my darling. We'll think of many more things for you to collect while you're home."

All the while we were talking, Nina remained seated, listening intently to our conversation. Her one hand gripped the edge of the table while the other encircled the baby on her lap. Finally, she stood and faced Mama. "I'll help in any way I can, Mrs. Sternik."

Mama smiled faintly. "Thank you, Nina. I'm not sure what you're going to be able to do. And I'm worried that it may become against the law for you to work for a Jewish family."

"I'm not an employee," Nina replied. "I'm a friend."

I almost cried when she said that.

"Nevertheless," Mama continued, "I'll understand if you feel you have to leave—"

Nina interrupted. "As I said before, I am not going anywhere."

"Mama?" I asked. "If our country has been invaded, does that mean there are going to be soldiers in town? Are we going to be arrested?"

Mama closed her eyes. When she opened them a moment later, there was a look of determination on her face. She rose from the table and went over to the window, glancing up and down the street. Then she pulled the curtains closed, and as the light was sucked from the room, she turned to face us.

"I will never let that happen," she said. "From now on, we are all going to stay in the house all of the time."

"Not even the yard?" I asked.

"Not even the yard." Mama stared straight at me and Nadia as she said this. "I don't want to draw attention to ourselves."

"But how long are we going to have to stay indoors?" I asked.

"As long as we have to." Mama's words hung heavily in the air. She sighed deeply. "And now, I think I need to lie down."

With that, Mama disappeared into her bedroom.

Nina put the baby in her high chair and turned back to the kitchen. Our grandfather clock chimed out ten bells. It was only mid-morning and so much had already happened. I sat down beside Nadia, who had gathered some of her strings and was trying to twist them into a braid. I reached over to hold the ends so she could weave the strands together.

"We'll be able to do more of this now that we're both home," I said, trying to keep my voice light. "It'll be fun."

Nadia paused and looked up at me, a serious look on her face. "I understand what's happening, Dina."

"You do?" My voice caught in my throat.

She nodded. "There are lots of people who don't like us anymore just because we're Jewish."

"That's right."

She sighed. "They must not like themselves very much if they need to find other people to hate."

My eyes widened. It was such a wise comment coming from my little sister.

"I'm not a baby anymore," she added, catching my look. "I'm going to be seven soon."

I nodded again. Under any other circumstances, Nadia, at seven, would have still been a child. But not now. Not in this time. Not in this world.

CHAPTER 14

We stayed behind closed doors for a couple of weeks. The radio reports had said that Nazi troops were patrolling in every city in Ukraine. But as far as we knew, no soldiers had been near our house. Not that we could be absolutely sure, as we kept the curtains drawn. Mama would occasionally pull them apart to peek outside, which was the only time that natural light entered our home. I wouldn't have had any sense of whether it was day or night if it weren't for our grandfather clock, which continued to chime on the hour as if nothing had changed.

Nadia played with her string and thread, and when she ran out of those, she moved on to collecting bits of fabric and cloth that she pulled from Mama's sewing kit. She claimed she was making a quilt for one of her dolls. She lined up a patchwork of irregularly shaped cloth pieces that Nina was helping her sew together.

Mama's headaches were growing worse. I could tell in an instant when a headache was starting. First, her eyes would cloud over. Then her brow would crease and she would drop her head into her hands. Finally, she would excuse herself and retreat to her bedroom to try to sleep it off. I knew she was worried all the time. I figured that would make anyone's head hurt!

I spent most of my time reading, though it seemed as if I had already read every single book in the house and was starting to reread some. In between, I played with the baby, helped Nina, and tried to make each day pass as quickly as possible. It helped to have a schedule for myself: wake up early, breakfast, clear the dishes, stretching and exercises, reading, lunch, clean-up, play with the baby, read some more, dinner, clean up, and bedtime. But even with my schedule, there were still long stretches of time that moved slower than a turtle walking up a hill. Those were the worst times, and in those moments, I missed Esther desperately. I missed our time together at school, our conversations about anything and everything, our picnics in the park. All of it was gone. I didn't even know how Esther was, if she and her family were safe. And there was no way for me to find out.

The only bright spot came when the baby began to take her first steps. She had been pulling herself to a standing position for some weeks. And then one day, she just launched herself forward and waddled across the kitchen, her arms spinning in circles to help steady herself. We cheered and laughed and Mama threw her high in the air just like Papa used to do. It was a moment of celebration, and Galya squealed with delight as if she knew she had just done something really important.

After two weeks, food began to grow scarce in the house. Nina prepared soups and stews that magically stretched our provisions to last more than a few days. But the baby needed milk, and when the last drop of that was gone, Mama came to Nina with her purse in her hands.

"We're going to need some things to tide us over." She didn't say for how long and no one asked. "Nina, I'm going to have to ask you to go to the market for us."

"Is it safe for Nina to be outside?" I asked.

"Nina can go," Mama said to me. "If there are soldiers about, they won't be interested in a Christian woman." She turned back to Nina. "I just don't want you to talk about us—that is, if anyone asks."

"Of course I'll go," Nina said without a moment's

hesitation. "And I would never say a word about the family." She had already removed her apron and was walking to the door to get her shawl.

Mama followed and handed her several bank notes, shaking her head as she counted out the money. "We have to be so careful with our spending. Please, Nina, make sure you shop wisely and look for the best prices."

I disappeared into my bedroom, leaving Mama to discuss with Nina the items that we desperately needed. There was something I wanted Nina to do for me, and I knew I only had a few minutes before she would leave the house. I pulled some writing paper from a box in my cupboard, grabbed a pen, plopped down on my bed, and began to write furiously. When I emerged a few minutes later, Mama and Nina were just finishing up their conversation.

"I know which merchants to go to, and which ones to avoid. Don't worry, Mrs. Sternik." Nina was wrapping her shawl around her shoulders and tucking the money carefully into the pocket of her dress.

I waited until Mama had gone to sit at the table with Nadia. Then I approached Nina.

"I have something to ask you," I said softly. "You can say no, but I hope you won't."

She paused and waited. I could tell that Mama was

listening in to my conversation.

"I've written a letter to Esther," I continued. "Do you think you'd be able to go past her house and drop it off?"

"I don't think that's a good idea," Mama interjected from the table. "I want Nina to come straight back here after she goes to the market."

"Esther's house is practically on the way," I said to Mama. Then I turned back to Nina. "As I said, you don't have to do this if it's not safe." I looked into Nina's eyes and waited, holding my breath, hoping. She turned the letter over in her hands.

Finally, Nina placed the letter in her pocket and looked at Mama. "I won't do anything foolish, Mrs. Sternik. If I think it's too dangerous, then I won't go." Finally, Nina looked at me. "I'll try."

I waited anxiously the whole time Nina was gone. I paced the length of the house, back and forth at least a hundred times, until Mama finally stopped me.

"Please, my darling. You'll wear a hole in the floor if you continue to pace like that. Nina will be fine. Just do something."

I sighed and went to my bedroom. There, I flopped down on my bed and opened one of my books. But I couldn't focus and I ended up rereading the same page over and over until I finally tossed the book aside and just lay there.

Mama had said that Nina was safer outside than any of us or any Jewish person could be, but we knew nothing of what the Nazis had on their minds: who they might target, or what they might do to any citizen of Proskurov. What if Nina didn't come back at all? We needed her more than ever, now. On top of that, I was nervous about Esther and what was happening to her. Maybe I had been wrong to ask Nina to deliver the letter to my friend. Maybe it was selfish of me to want information about Esther when I might be putting Nina in more danger. I turned those thoughts and others over and over in my head as the minutes ticked by to the sound of our grandfather clock.

When I heard the front door open, I flew out of my room, relieved and thankful to see Nina. She carried a small parcel of food, which she set on the kitchen counter. Then she removed her shawl. I was practically jumping out of my skin, anxious to hear what had happened in town.

"Tell us what you saw," Mama finally asked.

Nina's face, when she looked up at us, was pale, almost as white as Mama's was when she was at the peak of one of her headaches. Nina pressed her hands together in front of her mouth and took a deep breath.

But when she began to speak, her voice shook.

"There are no Jewish people anywhere in the marketplace," she began. "No Stars of David to be seen on any clothing. I think your whole community has disappeared behind closed doors."

Everyone had likely shut themselves away, just like us. "And soldiers?" I asked. "Did you see any?"

Nina nodded. "They were everywhere. They were carrying guns and they walked around as if they owned the city."

Nina said there was less and less food in the marketplace, and citizens were desperate for anything they could get.

"There were long lines in front of every stall and every shop—lines that were twenty or thirty deep," she said. "But the soldiers didn't care about the queues. They didn't care that people had lined up at the crack of dawn and had been waiting for hours to buy a loaf of bread or a liter of milk. They just shoved people aside, even women who were standing there with their babies in their arms. The soldiers grabbed whatever they wanted. They didn't pay. They just took, as if they owned it all." Nina's voice was graver than I had ever heard it. "No one stopped them. No one dared."

The silence in the room stretched for minutes.

"I stayed far away from Mrs. Timko," Nina finally continued. "I thought that she might ask whether or not I was still working for you. I worried she might make trouble. But I managed to get a bit of milk for the baby and a few other things for the rest of us. I'm not sure how long they will last. And I'm not sure what will be left in the market if I go back."

Those words hung uneasily in the air. Mama's face was pale, like she was starting to get one of those headaches.

"Thank you, Nina," she finally said. Then she just picked up the baby and disappeared into her bedroom, as if she couldn't bear to be part of the conversation any longer. Nadia left her patches of fabric and went to sit in a corner of the room. She pulled her knees up to her chest and rested her forehead against them. I felt just as discouraged and hopeless as she looked. But I needed to know—had Nina delivered my letter? I looked at her, waiting, wondering. That's when she reached into her pocket.

"This is from Esther," she said, pulling out an envelope and extending it to me. "I waited while she wrote an answer to your letter."

I threw my arms around Nina and hugged her hard. I was just about to retreat to my bedroom with the letter when she stopped me.

"There's one more thing." She went over to the counter and rummaged in the package she had carried home. When she turned back to me, she was holding a book in her hand. "I also went by the library. I thought you could use something else to read."

I nearly cried when she placed the book in my hands. It was another Heidi story—one that I hadn't read. I pressed it to my chest, unable to say a word. Then I turned and walked into my room, sank down on my bed, and tore open the envelope to read the letter from Esther.

Dear Dina,

I was so happy when your housekeeper arrived with your letter. I've missed you too! I can't believe we haven't been able to see each other and haven't been able to talk. So, to answer your first question: we are safe and as fine as we can be, for now. My father is doing a bit of tailoring here and there so he can make a little money. And one of our neighbors—a kind elderly woman—is buying us food from the market. So, we're not starving!

Do you believe everything that's happening, Dina? My parents don't talk much about it, but they cer-

tainly aren't as positive as they used to be. I can see how worried they are now. And I'm just as scared. I can be honest with you about that. I wish you were here so that we could talk. You're so much braver than I am. You're the one who stood up to Ivan and to Mr. Petrenko. I could never have done that.

I know your housekeeper wants to get going, so I'd better end this letter. Maybe she'll bring me another one from you if she goes back to the market. Stay safe, Dina. I know that my parents aren't thinking that things will go back to the way they were. But I'm going to keep hoping that all this will end soon. We'll see one another. We'll go back to school. I'll race you to the park. I can't wait for that.

Esther

I must have reread that letter a dozen more times before finally tucking it under my pillow.

CHAPTER 15

Nina went out the following week to buy more food. I gave her another letter for Esther, but this time she couldn't deliver it—there were soldiers patrolling in that area, she said, and she didn't want to draw attention to Esther's house. But she did come back with another book for me. I had devoured the first one in one sitting. I knew I needed to force myself to slow down when I read; I wasn't sure when Nina would be able to go out again, and even if she did, I wasn't sure she'd make it to the library. But it was nearly impossible to limit myself to a chapter or two when there was nothing else to occupy my time and my mind.

For the first time, Mama glimpsed soldiers on the street outside our house when she peeked through the curtains. She warned me to stay away from the window, but I couldn't resist. When she was resting in her bedroom, I stole a few glances outside. I saw a troop of soldiers pass, wearing ugly gray uniforms and carrying rifles over their shoulders. They had helmets like round metal bowls perched on the tops of their heads. They paused right in front of our house. I thought they might even be looking our way, their faces stone cold and unsmiling.

I shrank back from the window, shaking from head to toe, and wishing for a moment that I had listened to Mama and never looked outside in the first place. I could still hear the clomp, clomp, clomp of their black boots on the pavement as they finally marched away. I knew that those images and those sounds would stay with me, like the scar I had on my knee from the time I had fallen on sharp glass and cut myself. The bleeding had stopped, and the scar had faded eventually. But a faint outline was always there—a constant reminder of the injury.

"Come away from the window." Nina broke into my thoughts and came over to stand next to me. I saw her catch the look on my face.

"I just had to see what's going on," I whispered. "Those soldiers ..."

"We don't know what's happening. And looking outside doesn't help."

"But why are they here, Nina?"

She glanced at the curtained window and shook her head. "I wish I knew." And then she changed the subject. "Come and help me prepare something to eat. It'll take your mind off what's going on out there."

I nodded, grateful for the distraction.

The grandfather clock had just chimed six bells and I was washing some cabbage in the sink when I first smelled it—a distinct odor like burnt toast or logs cracking in the hearth. Nina hadn't started the stove yet, and there was nothing burning in the fireplace. Perhaps the neighbor down the way was burning some leaves outside and the smell was wafting toward us.

I went back to washing cabbage and began to think about writing another letter to Esther. Perhaps the next time Nina went out, she would be able to deliver this one and wait for another reply. Nina had said that soldiers were patrolling in Esther's neighborhood as well. I wondered if she had seen them too.

The smell in the room wasn't going away. In fact, it seemed to be getting worse. And when I turned away from the sink, I could see a layer of smoke that hung in the room like a low cloud on an overcast day. A second later, Mama burst from her bedroom holding the baby up against her chest.

"Fire!" she screamed. "The house is on fire!"

At first, I didn't move. I couldn't. My feet seemed stuck to the floor, as if they'd been glued there. And my head felt as cloudy as the smoke in the room that was growing thicker by the second.

"Fire!" Mama screamed again as she tore through the house.

I still couldn't move. And then, a second later, Nina stood in front of me. She grabbed me by my shoulders and shook me hard, staring straight into my eyes.

"Get Nadia," she commanded. "We need to get out of the house. Now!"

The shaking finally brought me back to my senses. I blinked once, nodded, and then ran for my sister. She was sitting in a corner of the living room—the spot that had become a refuge for her in the days since we had been barricaded indoors. Her arms were wrapped around her knees and she stared, wild-eyed, at the chaos that was playing out in our house as the smoke continued to thicken.

"Nadia!" I didn't want to scream, didn't want to frighten her any more than she already looked. But it was hard to keep my voice even when my heart was thumping so loud in my chest and my lungs felt as if they might explode.

I pulled Nadia up, dragged her to the door, and

looked back at Mama. She had given the baby to Nina and was running around the house, opening cupboards and muttering under her breath, "What should we take? What do we need?"

Nina had already collected a bit of food in a basket and was standing next to me at the door with the baby in her arms. "We have to leave, Mrs. Sternik. Please! We must go!"

"Yes, yes." Mama was still pacing from one corner of the room to the other, her eyes casting about, unseeing, her hands thrown up in the air as if in surrender.

That was when I shrieked as loud as I could, "Mama! We need to get out of here!"

She finally stopped, raised her head, and ran to join us. We all grabbed arms and bolted out the door.

We didn't stop running until we'd reached the end of our street. There, we turned to look back at our house. The sight that greeted me made my jaw drop. Smoke billowed in massive clouds from the roof, exploding like lava and pouring across the sky. The flames followed, rising higher and higher, glowing in the early evening twilight. Deep red, orange, and yellow—colors that I had loved in the past but that suddenly filled me with horror.

And the sounds! I had never imagined that a fire

could be so noisy. Timber splintered. Glass shattered. Paint crackled. The sounds combined, growing ever louder into a painful chorus that pounded inside my head. The smell was next—so strong and foul that it made my eyes water. I coughed and gagged.

"Cover your faces. Try not to breathe in," Mama shouted.

"My treasures," Nadia suddenly screamed, taking a step back toward the house.

"Nadia, stop!" Mama reached out and grabbed her, pulling her close. Nadia thrashed and struggled in Mama's arms.

"But all my collections are going to get burnt up!" Nadia cried, trying to get away from Mama, and then finally sinking back in her arms.

I too couldn't help but picture all of our things crumbling into nothing: the dresser in the sitting room where I had hidden as a child; the table in the kitchen where we had eaten all of our meals and where my birthday cake had magically appeared each year; the swing in the backyard where I had held the baby and pumped her up and down; the letter from Esther; all my lovely books—everything curling up in the flames and disappearing into nothing but ash.

"They're just things," Mama said, watching me. But when I looked over at her, her eyes were red and brimming with tears.

"Papa's portrait," I whispered. "And the grand-father clock—your mother's heartbeat."

That's when Mama's face crumbled like the build-ing in front of us, and she looked back in anguish.

Yes, they were just things and didn't compare with our safety. But each item in the house had been like a friend, holding the memory of a special time. I couldn't bear the thought that they were all gone.

"Don't look," Mama said. "It's best not to look." But her eyes were glued to the house, unable to turn away.

Tears were streaming down Nina's face. I real-ized it was the first time I had ever seen her cry. She clutched the baby so tightly in her arms that Galya finally gave a yelp and tried to wriggle free. Nina soft-ened her grip.

I looked frantically in both directions. The neigh-boring houses were some distance away, but it didn't appear as if any other house was on fire. Just ours. That was when I thought about the soldiers I had seen patrolling past our house earlier in the day. There was no sign of them now. Had they had anything to do with this?

"Will the fire trucks come?" I cried.

Mama also looked up and down the road. Then

she turned back to me. From the defeated look on her face, I knew that no one was coming to help us. We were all alone.

CHAPTER 16

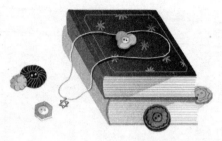

There was only one place Mama could think of for us to go, and that was to Papa's brother, my uncle, who had married a Christian woman and disappeared from our lives. I wasn't sure I wanted to go to him. It seemed pretty clear that he hadn't wanted anything to do with us. He hadn't even come to Papa's funeral, although Mama had told him about it.

"We have nowhere else to go," Mama said as the flames from our house finally began to die down and turn back into black smoke.

I nodded reluctantly, grabbed Nadia's hand, and followed Mama and Nina, who was still holding the baby. We walked through darkened streets, heads down, huddling close to one another until we finally arrived at a small brick house in a neighborhood I had never been in before. Mama said that few Jewish people lived here. When we knocked, it took several minutes for the lights to come on. Finally, a woman answered, shrinking back when she saw us.

We must have been quite a sight standing there on the darkened doorstep. Our faces were smeared with smoke and ash. Our clothes were just as dirty. Even Nina's pink scarf was stained with soot. Mama clutched my arm and Nadia's. Nina stood behind her holding the baby.

"Maria, it's me, Frima Sternik," Mama began. "You remember us, of course."

I looked curiously at this stranger who was my uncle's wife. She was thin as a rake with shoulders that curled forward into her chest. Her hair was wrapped in a tight scarf—like Nina's, I thought, except that Maria's scarf was gray. The creases in her forehead looked as if they had been stamped there permanently. She shrank back from us even more, wrinkling her nose as she looked us up and down. I'm sure we smelled as nasty as we looked.

"What do you want?" she asked. There was another look in her eyes mixed with the disdain. She looked afraid.

Mama opened her mouth to speak, but then she just stopped. It was as if the nightmare of the fire suddenly overwhelmed her. She squeezed her eyes shut.

That's when Nina stepped forward.

"I'm Ludviga Pukas," she began. "I'm with the Sternik family."

Then Nina began to explain about the fire that had taken us by surprise and destroyed our home.

Suddenly, a man appeared behind Maria in the doorway. I gasped. He looked so much like Papa—the same strong chin, the same fair hair and blue eyes, the same broad shoulders. Seeing my uncle was like staring at Papa's ghost. When he spoke, he had the same calm voice.

"Come in," he said. "Come in at once."

Maria put her arm on his. "Leo, what are you doing? It's dangerous to have them here." She poked her head out the door and glanced up and down the street.

"It's much more dangerous to keep them on the doorstep," my uncle replied. "We need to let them in."

"Our house burned down," I said, my voice hoarse from the smoke.

My uncle stared at me and then back at his wife. She looked as if she was going to say something more. But finally, she looked away and stepped aside.

I glanced around as we entered the house. It was neater than any place I had ever seen—not a book or a plate or a chair that was out of place. I knew that my uncle and his wife had no children, and I wondered what they would do if Nadia were to bring one of her collections into their spotless surroundings. Then I remembered that Nadia had no collections and no treasures left. We had nothing. Our home was gone.

My uncle's wife was still staring at us. I patted down my hair and tugged nervously on my skirt. Mama was the one who finally spoke.

"Thank you for taking us in, Maria. Might we be able to wash up?"

My uncle's wife nodded and directed us to a bathroom.

I barely recognized myself when I looked into the small mirror that hung above the sink. My face was smudged with dirt and my blond hair was streaked with soot. There was a big tear in the sleeve of my blouse, and my Star of David hung from a single thread; I didn't even know how or when that had happened. Mama and Nina were taking turns scrubbing Nadia and the baby in the tub behind me. I bent over the sink and splashed cool water on my face, holding my hands there for a moment and breathing in and out, trying to calm my heart that was still racing. Just then, there was a soft knock at the door. When Mama opened it, Maria was standing there with a bundle in her hands.

"I managed to find some things for you to wear," she said, holding the bundle out to Mama. "There are nightgowns here as well as some things for tomorrow."

"You're very kind," Mama said, reaching out to accept the pile. My aunt turned and left before Mama could say another word.

When we finally returned to the kitchen, Maria had put some food out on the table for us—slabs of cheese and ripe tomatoes along with slices of bread and a tub of butter. I suddenly realized how hungry I was. I couldn't even remember the last time I had eaten. I devoured everything in sight under Maria's watchful eye. We all ate in silence, Nina quietly looking over at me and my sisters every few seconds as if she needed to check that we were still okay.

After we ate, Maria cleared the dishes, and Nina offered to make tea for everyone. The baby's eyes were drooping and Nadia rested her head on her arms atop the table. When Nina finished serving tea, she took my sisters to bed. I also longed to sleep—to try to shed the memory of everything that had just happened to us. My arms ached and my legs felt like dead weights. But I knew that Mama needed to talk to my uncle and Maria, and I needed to know what was going to happen to us. When Nina rejoined us a

few minutes later, Mama looked over at me. For a moment I thought she might ask me to leave, thinking I
was too young to be part of this conversation. But she
didn't say a word. She turned to my uncle and wasted
no time getting to the point.

"We have nowhere to go, Leo, and no one to turn
to."

My uncle nodded. "I heard that the Nazis are tar-
geting Jewish families. It was probably one of their
units that set fire to your house—or some of the thugs
in town who they've convinced to go along with
them."

"I saw soldiers walking by our house, Mama," I
said. "Earlier today."

My mother didn't know I had been looking out
our window. But she didn't flinch when I said this—
just nodded.

"What is it that you want from us?" Maria asked.
Her voice didn't sound as sharp as it had when we ar-
rived. But it still didn't seem as if she wanted to help.
Mama looked at her and then back at my uncle.

"You are my husband's brother," she said. "We are
your family. And we need your help."

My uncle exhaled a long slow breath. "What can
we do?"

"Let us stay here," Mama said. "I promise it won't

be for long. I'll start looking for another place for us to live tomorrow."

"You know it's not going to be easy to find something," Maria interjected. "Jews are not wanted in any neighborhood."

I stared at her when she said this. She caught my eye and then turned away.

My uncle sighed again. "You can stay for as long as you need to," he said.

Maria looked at my uncle, opened her mouth as though to object, and then clamped it shut. Finally, she rose from the table, put the last of the dishes away, and left the room. My uncle reached up to rub his eyes. Then he leaned forward to stare at Mama.

"I'm sorry I haven't been a better brother-in-law to you." He turned to me. "Or a better uncle to you and your sisters."

I stared at him, realizing there was so little that I knew of his circumstances and his life. Had he decided to reject his Jewish faith and all of us when he married my aunt? Or had she turned him against us? Or was it my family who had pushed him away?

"And you mustn't be angry with my wife," he added. "She's just scared."

"We're scared, too." The words were out of my mouth before I realized what I was saying.

Nina just sat with her head down, saying nothing.

My uncle looked at me sadly. "Yes, I can imagine you are," he finally said.

CHAPTER 17

My head felt heavy when I woke up the next morning. I had had trouble falling asleep. Every time I closed my eyes, visions of smoke-filled rooms entered my brain. Flames consumed my mind. I felt as if I was choking again, gasping for air and feeling like my lungs were being sucked dry. Light was already starting to creep into the room when I finally fell asleep.

I sat up slowly and rubbed my eyes. That was when the memory of the previous day flooded through me again. We had lost our house. We had lost everything. And even though we were lucky that my uncle was allowing us to stay here for now, I had no idea where we were going to live or what was going to happen to us. And all of that was made so much worse for the fact that we were Jewish and no one wanted anything to do with us.

Nadia and the baby were snoring softly next to me, sprawled across the bed, their faces at peace, as if nothing bad had just happened to them. I wished I could feel the way they looked. Mama and Nina were deep in conversation at the other end of the room. I could tell from the way their heads were bent toward one another and from their whispered tone that they probably didn't want me to hear what they were saying. But I figured that the time for secrets was long past. We had been through enough together.

Mama turned and caught me staring at her. "Oh, you're up," she said. "We didn't wake you, did we?"

I shook my head. "I didn't sleep very much."

She nodded sympathetically.

"What are you talking about?" I asked.

Mama exchanged looks with Nina.

"Tell me, Mama," I insisted.

Mama sighed. "We're going to have to go to the authorities today. All of our papers were lost in the fire. And unless we're registered and have identity documents, we'll never be able to get a new home."

"But where *are* we going to live, Mama?" *Jews are not wanted in any neighborhood.* That's what Maria had said.

Mama suddenly looked as tired as I was feeling. Her shoulders drooped and she shook her head.

"I don't know. What I do know is that we can't stay here for long. We just need to find a couple of rooms somewhere. How hard can that be?" She looked at Nina as she said this.

"You said it yourself, Mrs. Sternik," Nina replied. "As long as we're together—that's what's most important. Everything else will work itself out."

We dressed in the clothes that my aunt had given us the day before. Mama and Nina wore simple smocks. I put on a pair of loose-fitting trousers and a sweater. There was a dress for Nadia and some baby clothes for Galya. There was even a scarf for Nina to wrap around her hair, a gray one that I thought must have come from my aunt. I had no idea where Maria had gotten the rest of the clothes for us, but I was grateful to have something that didn't smell like the fire.

My uncle was in the kitchen when we sat down to have some breakfast, but my aunt was nowhere to be seen.

"A headache," my uncle murmured when Mama asked after her. Then he quickly set out bread, milk, and jam on the table for us. Nina boiled water for tea and after helped clear away the dishes and wash the table and floor. My uncle looked at her gratefully.

"We're going to the county office today," Mama

explained to my uncle when we had finished cleaning up. "I want us to be out of here as soon as possible. And out of your wife's way."

My uncle opened his mouth as if he were going to object. But instead he said, "Just be careful." He indicated our clothing. "The Nazis may have taken over the county office by now. And you're not wearing any stars. If anyone on the street recognizes you, or if the authorities figure out that you're Jewish, you'll be in big trouble."

I hadn't even thought of that! All of our clothing had burned up in the fire along with all of the Stars of David that we had carefully stitched onto them. I reached up to touch the spot on my blouse where the star was meant to be.

Mama nodded wearily. "I'm aware of that. But what choice do we have? We have to get new documents if we're going to be able to get a new place to live. And for that, we have to go to the county office. And we all have to go in person—even the children."

"Will we be arrested?" I asked nervously.

Nadia's face went pale. "Are we going to jail, Mama?" she asked.

"No, my darlings," Mama replied without a moment's hesitation. "That will never happen."

"Come, Nadia," Nina said. "Let's get your shoes on

and you can help me get the baby ready for our outing." She took my sister by the hand and went back
into the bedroom. When they were out of earshot,
Mama turned back to my uncle.

"Nobody on this side of town knows us. And we'll
avoid any place where we might be recognized." She
paused. "It's the only solution."

We took a long route to the county office, avoiding
any familiar streets. Still, the longer we walked, the
more on edge I felt. With each person we passed,
I worried more and more about being recognized.
Did that woman know us? I wondered as someone
brushed by me on the busy road. Did that man just
look our way? I fretted as someone else glanced in our
direction. I tried to keep my head down, held Nadia's
hand firmly, and followed closely behind Mama. Nina
carried the baby in her arms and walked behind us.
She seemed to be lagging, and at one point, I turned
to look at her.

"Hurry up, Nina," I urged. The quicker we got
there, the quicker we'd be off the street and hopefully
out of danger.

It was as if Nina didn't hear me. She continued
to trail behind, plodding along slowly. Suddenly, she
picked up her pace and strode quickly past me, catch-

ing up to Mama as if I wasn't there.

"Mrs. Sternik, I have to talk to you."

"We've got to keep moving, Nina." Mama didn't slow for one second. But Nina would not be put off.

"Please," she continued. "It's important. I have to tell you something before we get to the county office."

At that, Mama finally slowed down. "Yes, what is it?"

Nina looked intently at Mama before she spoke. "I don't know if the authorities will give you a new place to live if you tell them that you and the children are Jewish."

Mama stared at Nina. "But we're entitled to a new place after a disaster like the fire. I know that's the case."

"That may have been the case in the past. But your brother-in-law said he thought that the Nazis had taken over the county office. He also said that they were the ones who probably burned down the house. If that's true, then why would they give you a new one?"

As that realization began to sink in, Mama's face went pale. "Oh, no! You're absolutely right."

And in that moment, something occurred to me. "Nina's right, Mama," I said. "We can't tell the authorities that we're Jewish. If we do, then how will you explain that we aren't wearing our stars?" I brought my hand up to my chest as Mama's face turned even whiter. She squeezed her eyes shut.

"But what can we do?" she whispered. "What can we do?"

It was an impossible situation. We had been targeted by the Nazis because we were Jewish. And now, we couldn't tell them our religion or we would be targeted again. But we needed new identity documents in order to get a new place to live. And we couldn't get those papers unless we identified ourselves. My thinking went around and around in never-ending circles. We were in a deep hole and it appeared that there was no escaping it.

"I can't seem to think," Mama said fretfully, shaking her head.

"I have an idea," Nina said. Then she stepped even closer to Mama and began to talk in a low and urgent voice. The words flowed out of her in one long stream. She didn't stop and she didn't take a breath. And when she finished, she stepped back and waited.

"I don't know …," Mama began. She bit her lower lip and shook her head.

"I think it's the only solution," Nina said. "But it will mean everyone needs to understand what they must do."

Mama looked as if she was thinking hard, weighing everything Nina had said. Then she looked at me. "Do you think it will work?"

I had to admit that Nina's idea sounded crazy, and incredibly dangerous. But it was also good, and probably the only chance we had. I glanced at Nadia. She was staring, eyes bulging, and taking it all in. "Nadia," I said. "Do you understand what we're asking you to do? What we're all going to have to do?"

She nodded solemnly.

"We're going to have to pretend—like real actresses," I said. "Can you do that?"

She nodded again. "I keep telling you I'm not a baby anymore."

Finally, I looked back at Mama and said, "We'll make it work."

CHAPTER 18

Up ahead, I could see long banners hanging from the county office building, adorned with that same swastika that I had seen on the sign barring Esther and me from the park—a jet-black symbol against a blood-red flag. I must have stiffened or slowed my step as we approached because Mama whispered, "Don't stare," and then gently nudged me forward. Still, the sign and that symbol made my blood run cold. My uncle was right: the county office had been taken over by the Nazis. But I could see no Nazi soldiers in those ugly uniforms, like the ones who had marched by our house a day earlier. And for that, I gave a silent prayer of thanks. Instead, several men in suits stood leaning against the building as we climbed the stairs to the front door. When these men saw the group of us trudging up the stairs in single file—two women and several children in tow—one man rushed to open the door, bowing slightly as we passed. He looked at me and, without thinking, my hand reached up again to brush across the place on my blouse where a Star of David should have been sewn. The man didn't react, and I quickly withdrew my hand.

Inside, we made our way down the hallway, following a sign pointing the way to the registry office. There was a long line out the door, but I didn't pay attention to who was waiting ahead of us. My eyes were lowered to the floor and I said nothing as the line inched forward. My stomach was doing flip-flops. All of a sudden, Nina's good idea seemed so harebrained, so far-fetched, that I believed it would never work. That thought very nearly made me sick. We were going to be discovered, and who knew what might happen to us then. But there was no other choice. We had come this far and had to keep going.

Nina now stood at the front of our group. Nadia and I stood on either side of her with Mama just behind, holding the baby. Suddenly, we were at the front of the line, and a man at a small desk in a corner of the room waved us forward. Nina went first and we followed. The man, wearing a dark suit and looking bored, barely glanced up at us. "Yes?"

A long moment passed while no one replied. I

felt a moment of panic as I glanced at Nina. Had she forgotten everything that we had discussed outside, everything that she was meant to do? But no—her face was calm and determined, as if she was weighing up the situation and figuring out what she needed to say. The official looked up.

"What do you want? I don't have all day?" He pushed up his glasses that had been perched on the end of his nose, and stared at us.

"My home burned down in a fire and all our papers were lost," Nina finally said in a voice that shook a little but was clear. And then she swept her hand over my head and that of my sisters. "These are ..." She paused and then began again in a steadier voice. "These are my children and I need to register all of us, again."

I stared at the official. This was the idea that Nina had proposed to Mama. She would claim to be our mother. If she could convince the official that we were all good Catholic citizens of Proskurov, then she would be able to get new identity papers for us, and she hoped that would entitle her to a new home.

As much as I had wanted to go along with her idea—it was probably the only chance we had—I knew that there were so many things that could go wrong. What if the official looked further into where we had lived? It wouldn't take much for this man to find out that the house that had burned down belonged to a Jewish family with three children and not this weathered-looking woman with a gray scarf tied tightly around her head. What if he questioned us further and Nadia forgot to pretend that Nina was now her mother? My younger sister had promised that she could play along, but in front of this stern-looking man would she be able to carry it off? What if the baby chose this moment to begin to talk? She was still just babbling sounds that made no sense. But what if she suddenly reached out for our mother and said "Mama!" What if someone we knew walked into the office at this very moment and recognized us? On and on, the disastrous scenarios played themselves out in my brain. None of it was making me feel better. My stomach was lurching and tumbling, and I was suddenly afraid I'd be sick on the spot.

In the meantime, Nina seemed more and more composed. She pulled her shoulders back, lifted her chin, and folded her hands in front of her. She looked calmer than I had ever seen. Mama stood behind all of us, ready for us to make a run for it if anything went wrong.

Sweat was gathering under my arms. I breathed in and out, trying to steady myself. And then I reached up again and rubbed my blouse and the place where a star should have been. I felt my face grow warm, as if I was standing in front of the fire that had consumed our home a day earlier.

But instead of questioning us, the bored-looking official simply reached into his desk drawer and pulled out some papers. "There are so many problems with so many houses, I can hardly keep up with the paperwork," he mumbled under his breath. "I don't know what's going on anymore. And no one tells me anything." He held the document out to Nina. "Write your name and the names of your children here and here. Then write your religion here." He indicated several spaces on the paper.

I heard Mama gasp behind me and I knew instantly what she must be thinking—she had no idea that I'd taught Nina to read or write! Our secret was suddenly out in the open, and not in a way that we had planned. I whirled around to face Mama. Our eyes locked, mine pleading with her to stay still, and hers looking confused and uncertain. Instinctively, she took a step forward. But just then, Nina spoke up again.

"Do you have a pen, please?"

Mama froze and looked even more puzzled than before. The county official rummaged in his desk for a pen and passed it to Nina, who leaned over the paper and, with a steady hand, began to print her name in capital letters. LUDVIGA PUKAS. Underneath, she wrote our new names: ELDINA PUKAS, GENNADIY PUKAS, GALYA PUKAS. Then she scanned down the paper and next to the word *religion*, she wrote CATHOLIC. She didn't hesitate for one second, even as Mama's mouth gaped open.

"Who's that one?" The official peered over his glasses at Mama, who was still open-mouthed.

"My housekeeper," Nina said without skipping a beat.

"And her name?"

Nina paused, and my heart began to race once more. This was something we had not prepared for or thought through. Was everything going to fall apart now?

"Her name," the official demanded once more.

I looked up at Nina, her face still calm and composed. "Her name is Daria Melnik."

I had no idea where this name had come from or how Nina had come up with it on the spur of the moment.

"I need all the help I can get with these three young ones," Nina added. "My housekeeper will need a new identity document as well." Then she bent over the paper once more and wrote Mama's new name on a separate line. She added the word CATHOLIC next to that as well.

"When do you think we might get our papers and a new place to live?" Nina asked as she passed the paper back to the official. "I've got to settle these three as quickly as possible. You can imagine how difficult all this has been for us."

Nina appeared to be growing more and more comfortable in her new role.

The county official reviewed the document and then reached for an ink pad and stamp, bringing the stamp down on the paper with a loud thump. "A couple of days should do it. I'll have your new papers and a furnished apartment ready for you." He glanced up, looking at Nadia and me and pushing his glasses up on his nose one more time. "I've got three of my own," he added. He appeared to be less bored and more interested in us now. "My wife does most of the work, of course, but she practically throws the kids at me when I get home at night. If I'd known how much work three was going to be, we'd never have had them. I must say, I admire anyone who can raise children alone, even with a housekeeper's help."

We had been in this office long enough. I knew it was time to get out of there before this man became too talkative and too curious about us. I reached over and took Nina's arm.

"Mama," I said loudly and clearly. "I think we need to go before the little ones get hungry. Don't you think?"

The official nodded at me. "Looks like that one is helpful at least."

And then Nadia took a step forward and grabbed Nina's other arm. "Yes, Mama, let's go."

At that, Nina smiled, and I realized I hadn't seen that smile in a long while. Her dimple deepened as she turned back to face the official. "Yes," she said. "They are both very helpful."

CHAPTER 19

We didn't say a word until we were far away from the county office building. Mama was the first one to break the silence.

"Wherever did you learn to read and write, Nina? I thought we were finished when that man asked you to write our names down."

Nina, who had appeared so confident during the entire time we were in the county office, suddenly looked embarrassed and awkward. She lowered her head and then looked up at me. "Perhaps you should tell your mother," she said.

"Tell me what?" Mama asked.

"I've been teaching her," I said. And then I explained the whole story to Mama—how we had read books together at the library almost every day after school. "When we were still allowed to go to school,"

I added. "Nina learned faster than anyone I know."

"But why didn't you tell me?" Mama asked.

Nina's face had gone bright red. "It was our secret—Dina's and mine. I knew I would tell you at some point, when it felt right. I didn't imagine you'd find out this way. You're not angry at me, are you, Mrs. Sternik?"

"Angry? I'm delighted!"

"Dina has been an excellent teacher," Nina added.

Now it was my turn to blush. But inside, I couldn't have felt prouder.

"Well, that certainly was a surprise. And thank goodness for it. The two of you saved the day for us in there." Mama pointed back at the county office.

"What about me, Mama?" Nadia asked, pulling on Mama's sleeve. "Didn't I save the day too?"

I reached down to hug my sister. "You were fantastic, Nadia. You pretended Nina was our mother, just like we explained. You were a great actress."

Nadia beamed. "I told you I understand things."

"Yes," Mama agreed. "You are certainly not a baby anymore."

There was still one thing I needed to know. "That name for Mama. Nina, where did you come up with it?"

"It was my late mother's maiden name," Nina explained. "It was the one name that popped into my head when that man asked who your mother was."

"How lucky for us that it did," Mama said.

Nina nodded. "I always feel as if my mother watches over me. I guess this was a time when she really did."

Nina beamed her giant smile that stretched from ear to ear. Mama smiled too, and then she began to laugh. I hadn't heard that sound come out of her in the longest time. A moment later Nadia joined in, and finally, me. Even the baby giggled along with us. We all walked together and laughed out loud. It felt good to laugh. It felt hopeful.

The man at the county office had said it would take a couple of days for our papers to be ready, along with a new apartment. Until then, we counted the hours and tried to stay out of my aunt's way as much as possible. She didn't try to talk to us and stayed in her bedroom most of the time. The only time she came out was to bring us another set of clothing, handing the items silently to Mama and then disappearing again into her bedroom. Once again, we had no idea where the clothes had come from, but Mama accepted them gratefully. My uncle helped us prepare meals and Nina helped tidy wherever she could. Everyone was on edge. Even the baby looked nervous. She clung to Mama or to Nina, not letting me or Nadia hold her. It was as if she also understood that she wasn't welcome in this house.

The same bored-looking official was at the county office when we finally returned. I worried that, in the intervening days, the Nazis might have taken more control of the situation and investigated our backgrounds. Would someone stop us this time? Would they know who we really were? Would they figure out that we had lied and arrest us? Luckily, my worries were unfounded. The official behind the desk barely looked up as he passed the new identity documents and keys over to us along with a piece of paper that listed the address of our new home. Then, he finally glanced up at us and pushed his glasses back up on his nose.

"That's all. You can go," he said, before calling for the next person in line.

We fled from there as fast as we could. Then we returned one last time to my uncle's house to say goodbye.

"Good luck to all of you," my uncle said, stepping forward to give an awkward embrace to my mother. Then he turned to me and said, "I do hope to see you again, Eldina."

I didn't answer. It was only when I felt a gentle nudge in the small of my back from my mother that I curtsied and replied, "Thank you."

My aunt had surfaced from her bedroom to watch us leave. She hovered behind her husband, her hands clenched in front of her, her eyes looking in every direction but ours.

Mama extended a hand to her. "Thank you for the clothes that you were able to find for us. And thank you for allowing us to stay here. I know it's been a difficult time for you, and we're grateful."

Maria stared at the hand for a long moment, and then reached up hesitantly to shake it. "Yes, well, good luck," she said.

My uncle moved to the door and then turned and pressed some money into Mama's hands. "It isn't much. I know you'll receive a small allowance from the county office. But perhaps this will also help you get by for the next little while."

Mama glanced down, a look of surprise on her face. "Oh," she stammered. "Thank you for this. It will help so much."

"Perhaps you'll try and stay in touch," my uncle said as we opened the door. "Just to let me know that you're safe."

"Yes, of course we will," Mama replied.

As we walked out, I believed it was the last time I'd ever see my uncle.

Our new apartment was on a pretty tree-lined street in a different part of the city from where we used to live, far from my uncle, far from the school Nadia and I had once attended, and far from any neighbors or acquaintances who might know us. That was a relief. Nina checked the address on the piece of paper we had been given and finally stopped in front of a small three-storey brick building. Flower boxes adorned several of the windows above us, overflowing with bright yellow sunflowers that turned their faces toward the sun. The branches of a tall oak tree hung over the building like a giant umbrella—so much like the tree that had stood in our backyard. A wave of sadness overcame me.

"This is it," Nina said.

We followed her up the stairs to the second floor and walked down a dimly lit hall. She stopped in front of a door with the number three on it. Then she took a deep breath and turned the key.

We entered into a small sitting room, sparsely furnished with a sofa and soft armchair. Next to it was a kitchen with a wooden table and four straight-back chairs. There were pots, pans, dishes, and cutlery, stored neatly in the cupboards and drawers. Long brown drapes that were partially drawn covered the windows. The apartment had two bedrooms off of the sitting room: one that would be for Mama and the baby, and one that I would share with Nina and Nadia. Several beds with pillows and blankets were set up in the bedrooms.

"It's good," Mama said as we finished moving through the space and investigating the cupboards and drawers. "In fact, it's perfect."

"I can make do with everything that's here, Mrs. Sternik," Nina added. "I'll have this looking like a cozy home in no time."

I smiled and nodded, even though I was thinking that this place felt cold and unwelcoming. Where were my books? Where was the grandfather clock ticking out the seconds and chiming on the hour? Where was Papa's portrait? Without those things, how could this place ever be our home?

Mama, sensing my thoughts, came over and placed her hands on either side of my face, drawing my forehead to touch hers. "We're together and we're safe. Isn't that what's most important?"

I nodded, and then Mama called the rest of the family together.

"We're fine while we're here in this apartment. But

out there"—she gestured out the window   "out there, nothing is very safe right now. As long as we're indoors you can continue to call me Mama. But if we ever go outside, you must remember to call me Daria. And out there, you have to refer to Nina as Mama." Her eyes swept over all of us. "Do you think you can do that?"

Nadia nodded solemnly. "I can do it, Mama. I did it before, when we were in that office."

"I know I can count on you, my darling," Mama replied.

I nodded as well. "You can count on me too."

"And me as well," Nina added.

Galya's eyes were as round as two apples as she stared at Mama, as though she too understood. We all stood silently for another few seconds, allowing the importance of our pact to sink in.

"How long do you think this is going to last?" I finally asked.

No one had an answer to that question, and Mama didn't even acknowledge it. Instead, she sighed and said, "Let's just try to get settled."

CHAPTER 20

There really wasn't very much to do to get settled in the small apartment. We had no luggage, no clothing, and no special belongings. Using some money from the allowance that the county office had given her, Nina went out to shop for us, traveling by tram across the city to the marketplace. There, she said she had kept her head down, shopped for the things we needed, and quickly got back onto a tram to come home. She bought a lamp for the bedroom, a small carpet for the sitting room, clothes that we desperately needed, and groceries that were even more important. She even bought a few colorful scarves for herself.

"I know I shouldn't spend the money on such silly things," she said, tying a bright green one around her head. "But it cost next to nothing. And I didn't feel like myself in that gray scarf that your aunt gave me."

I agreed! It almost felt as if things had returned to normal when I saw Nina wearing the same bright colors that she had worn before all the trouble began.

On one of her outings, she even found a small used bookstore and returned to the apartment with two books for me. I ran to my room and devoured them. I yearned for more and hoped Nina would continue to bring me books to read. I also longed for news of Esther, and to let her know that we were okay. I wanted to write her another letter and have Nina deliver it. But she couldn't bring herself to go past Esther's house.

"I can't take that chance," she said. "I couldn't tell Esther where we are. No one can know that. And there are only so many lies I can keep straight."

Of course, she was right. All I could do was pray that Esther and her family were as safe as we were.

Nadia started a collection of buttons that began to fill the windowsill of our bedroom. I was amazed at where my younger sister was able to find them— on the stairs leading up to our apartment, in the hall-way outside our door, even under the beds. Nadia, of course, was thrilled to have new *treasures*.

"You used to think I had too many things before," Nadia said one day as she lined up her buttons in order of size and color. "Aren't you glad that I have a new collection now?"

I had to admit that, with her growing assortment of buttons, it did feel as if our bedroom was becoming more familiar and cozier. I didn't even mind sharing the space with her. But I did yearn to get some fresh air. Mama refused to go outside, even though Nina encouraged her to do so.

"We need to look as if we're living here like normal citizens," she pleaded with Mama one day. Still, Mama said she was too nervous to be out in the open and afraid of anyone asking her questions. She stayed indoors and helped Nina take care of the apartment and us. She was equally nervous about me going outside and wanted to keep me and my sisters in her sight at all times. I had to admit that the thought of being in public scared me as well. But I was restless indoors all day, and the longing to be outside topped any fear I had.

"I won't go far," I said one day after we had been stuck in the apartment for several weeks. "I'll stay close by. And I'll come straight home if there's any trouble or anything that feels unsafe."

Mama wasn't convinced.

"It's summertime. No one will wonder why we're not at school," I added. That still didn't sway Mama, who continued to shake her head.

"The little ones need to get some fresh air, Mrs. Sternik," Nina said. "It's not healthy for them to be inside all the time. Besides, it will arouse suspicion if we lock ourselves away."

I thought that would persuade Mama for sure. But she still looked uncertain. "Maybe you should go with them, Nina," Mama said.

"I believe they'll be fine on their own," Nina replied. "You know how responsible Dina is—and Nadia. They won't do anything dangerous."

"You mustn't talk to anyone," Mama finally said to me.

"I won't."

"And only stay out for a few minutes."

She seemed to be giving in, and my hopes began to rise. "I promise, Mama."

Mama nodded her agreement. Her voice followed me and my sisters out the door. "Stay together. Stay close. Come back soon."

I turned and blew her a kiss and then, before she could change her mind, I grabbed the baby's hand to take her down the stairs. Nadia followed, her eyes trained on the ground to spot any buttons that she might add to her collection.

It was August, and summer had descended on

Proskurov in full force. The sun was a golden ball in the sky. The trees were heavy with leaves, their branches waving a warm greeting to me. I leaned my head back, closed my eyes, and breathed in deeply, smelling sweet roses and lemon and cut grass. There were several children across the road skipping with a jump rope. I longed to join them but I knew that was impossible. Too many questions. Too many lies to keep. Too dangerous. Mama's warnings echoed in my ears as I continued walking past.

We had been out walking for some time and I knew we should probably get back. Nadia was lagging, still eyeing the ground for some treasures. "Slow down, Dina," she called. "I might miss the perfect button if we go too fast."

I slowed my step and bent down to tickle the baby. She giggled and held her arms up to me to pick her up. With each passing day, she was walking steadier and with more balance. She no longer looked as if the top of her body was connected to the bottom with a spring that made it wobble from side to side. But she still loved to be held. I hoisted her up into the air and she squealed even louder. Then I turned back to Nadia. "I can't wait for you all day," I called. "We need to get back." But Nadia wasn't listening. She was on a mission to find some buttons and nothing was going to stop her. I glanced up the road. A woman wearing a brightly flowered housedress was approaching. She looked straight at me, her eyes assessing me up and down. I quickly lowered my head, held tighter onto the baby, and turned to urge Nadia to speed up again.

"Nadia, let's go."

Something in my voice must have alarmed her. Nadia looked up, spotted the stranger ahead of us, and moved immediately to my side. As we passed each other, the woman reached out and touched my elbow. It brought me to a dead stop.

"You're the family that moved into our building last month," she began.

I glanced at the open expression on her face. She sounded more curious than suspicious. But her question made me nervous. She had noticed our family at a time when we were trying to stay invisible. I wasn't going to talk to her, but I knew I had to be polite. So, I nodded and curtsied, and then began to walk on.

"I'm Mrs. Sirko," she called after me. "Apartment one on the main floor. Perhaps you'd like to tell me your name?"

My heart began to pound, and I stopped walking. Mama had said that no one could be trusted. This stranger seemed harmless enough, but I didn't want to give her any information. At the same time, saying nothing would be even more suspicious.

I turned back to her. "I'm Dina," I said, and for a second time tried to move away.

"And your last name?"

Why was this woman being so nosy? What was she trying to find out? Did she really just want to meet her new neighbors, or was there something more to her questions?

I stopped again, and this time it was Nadia who answered. "Our last name is Pukas."

The woman glanced at my sister. "Pukas," she repeated. "Well, I hope you're not going to be too noisy—three children and all." She looked as if she wanted to say something more. But that was when the baby opened her mouth and wailed as if on cue. I shifted her to my other arm. "We're usually very quiet. But we have to go," I said to the woman. "The baby's hungry and probably tired."

She looked uncertain, but said nothing more as we walked away. Once we got back to our building, we ran up the stairs and into the apartment. Mama looked up from her sewing.

"Was everything okay?" she asked.

I glanced at Nadia and then nodded. "Everything was fine, Mama." Better not to worry her more than she already was, I reasoned. Nothing had happened out there. We were back safe and sound. Besides, she might never let us out again if I told her I had spoken to a stranger.

One day, Nina came home with a radio, which hissed and crackled as Mama turned the dial to find a clear station. When she finally found one, a news bulletin was underway. The announcer was listing countries that were now involved in the war that had been started by Adolf Hitler. Hungary, Albania, Slovakia, Lithuania, Latvia—all countries that were close to us in Ukraine, and all falling to Hitler's rule. At one point the voice of Hitler himself echoed through our sitting room, as he blamed Jews for all the problems that Germany was experiencing and promised to rid the world of every last one of us.

Mama sat with her head down during the entire news report, rocking back and forth, moaning softly whenever another country was mentioned or another angry rant from Hitler blasted from the radio. Nina looked just as distraught. I wanted to switch the radio off. It was better to know nothing than to hear these terrible announcements and to think that the war was all around us and closing in. I wanted the news report to end. I wanted silence in our sitting room. But the report went on and on. The last item had to do with our city.

"In local news," the announcer said, "all Jews of Proskurov have been ordered to move to the ghetto that has been established near the market on Kamenetsky Street. Those failing to report to the ghetto will be forcibly relocated." With that, he finally moved on to talk about the heat wave that was coming to our city. That's when Mama finally rose to switch the radio off and then sat down again, her hands clasped tightly in her lap.

There was silence in our sitting room. I knew what a ghetto was. Even before the fire had burned our house to the ground, I had heard radio reports of ghettos being established in other cities across Europe where Hitler was already in charge. *City prisons* is what Mama had called them—places where Jews were locked up behind barbed wire and fences and chains. And now, the Jews of my city were being ordered to go there—to a city prison that was being set up in the exact place where we had once shopped in the market.

"Mama?" I finally squeaked out. "Will we have to go to the ghetto?"

When she looked at me, her face was pale but calm. "We have new identities. This doesn't apply to us. We're safe right where we are."

CHAPTER 21

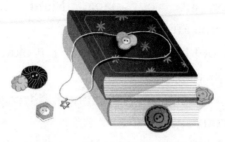

Mama came into my room that night as I was getting ready to go to bed. Nadia was already fast asleep, breathing evenly in the next cot. Nina was in the sitting room settling the baby and singing her a lullaby. Mama sank down onto my bed, saying nothing at first. Then, finally, she began to speak.

"The things that are happening out there to Jewish families like ours"—she gestured toward the darkened window—"they're all so upsetting and impossible to understand. Sometimes I think we'd be better off not knowing what's going on."

It was exactly what I had been thinking earlier.

"I try to sound positive when the little ones are around." She pointed at Nadia. "I don't want to scare them."

"Nadia understands more than you think she does."

"Yes, you're probably right. You've all had to grow up so fast—faster than you should have."

I didn't know where this was going.

"First you lost your papa," Mama continued. "Then our home and your friends."

I reached out to grab her hand. "I'm okay, Mama," I said. "I really am."

"You're so strong," she continued. "Stronger than I ever was at your age."

I didn't feel very strong these days, but Mama was sounding so serious, and I desperately wanted to lighten the mood. "At least Nina's with us," I said. "Do you remember how much I didn't want her to stay at first?"

At that, Mama smiled. "You barely even spoke to her when she came to live with us."

"You told me to be patient, but I didn't want to listen to you."

"I remember." Mama closed her eyes at the memory.

"I never told you this," I continued, "but I used to walk to school ahead of Nina because I didn't want anyone to know I had a babysitter. I didn't want anyone to think I needed someone to look after me."

"And look how much you love her now."

"She's a member of the family." I could hear Nina

singing softly to the baby in the next room.

"I don't know what we'd do without her," Mama agreed.

"We're lucky, Mama," I added. "All those people who have to move to the ghetto; we're so much luckier than they are. And you said it yourself; as long as we're together, we'll be okay."

Her face suddenly fell and she looked sadder than I had ever seen. "Yes, as long as we're together." Then she paused. "And I pray that will always be the case."

Mama was starting to worry me again. "Of course we'll be together."

She seemed not to hear me. "There's something that I want you to have—something that will always remind you of me," she said, reaching into the pocket of her dress.

"I don't need anything to remind me of you, Mama," I protested. "I have *you*."

"When our house was on fire," she went on, as though I hadn't spoken, "all I thought about was that we all had to get out of there safely. That was more important than any of the things that we owned. But I knew there was one piece of jewelry that I had to take with me. I grabbed this just before we ran out the door."

She held her closed fist out in front of her and

uncurled her fingers. There in her palm was a small Star of David suspended on a thin gold chain. I had never seen it before.

"Your papa gave it to me on the day we were married," Mama said. "But when you came along, I put it away in my jewelry box. I knew I would give it to you one day—my firstborn. I thought it would be on your wedding day." Tears were beginning to stream down Mama's cheeks. And I could feel a lump in my throat growing bigger by the second.

She held the necklace out to me. I hesitated a moment and then reached a shaky hand to take it from her, holding it up in the air and watching as the small star twirled around on its chain, catching the light with each turn. "It's beautiful," I exclaimed.

"I think that now is a good time for you to have this," Mama continued.

The weight of what she was saying began to sink in and I pushed the necklace back. "No, Mama!" I protested. "You keep it. I'm not getting married for years and years. I don't want it now."

Mama ignored my protests and placed the necklace back in my hands. "You will make me very happy if you take this."

I looked down at the star and then back at my mother.

"You won't be able to wear it during the day," she continued. "You know that you can't let anyone see that you're Jewish. But I thought you could wear it at night and then put it under your pillow during the day."

Taking a deep breath, I brought the necklace up and around my neck. But my hands were shaking so badly there was no way I could fasten it. Mama finally reached over to help me. When it was in place, she sat back and stared at me. "It looks perfect on you." She paused before continuing. "I want you to keep it with you always."

I fingered the small star and smiled at my mother, tears glistening in my eyes. "It's as if it's from you *and* from Papa."

"I'm so glad you understand," Mama said. "I knew you would. I'm always watching over you, and so is your papa." With that, she kissed me on the forehead and walked out of the room.

CHAPTER 22

I loved the necklace. I wore it every evening, fastening it around my neck and holding the Star of David gently in my hand as if it might break if I squeezed too tightly. And then every morning, I would unclasp it and place it under my pillow for safekeeping. I loved knowing it was there for me, waiting until the sun would set and I could wear it once again. Mama's face lit up every time she noticed it. It was as if the sight of the necklace soothed her. And that look of pleasure on Mama's face took away my fears.

But, when Mama didn't come home from the market a few days later, I knew something terrible must have happened. She shouldn't have even gone out that morning. She never left the apartment, despite my continued pleas, and Nina's, for her to at least take a walk on our street. But Nina had been feeling under the weather, and we desperately needed food, especially for the baby.

"Let me go," I said, trying to keep my voice down so I wouldn't wake Nina, who had taken to her bed. "I've been outside with Nadia and the baby. People in the neighborhood have seen me. They're used to seeing me on the street." That was true. I had continued to take my sisters for a walk most days. And we had been fine. Even the curious neighbor, Mrs. Sirko, who had asked so many questions the first day we had gone outside, only nodded hello if we saw each other on the street. She still looked as if she wanted to know more about us, but I just nodded back and continued on, never slowing to give her an opportunity to question me.

But Mama wouldn't hear of my plan. "It's too far for you to go to the market on your own."

"But it's far for you to go too." The market was across the city, and a tram ride away, back in our old neighborhood where we had not ventured since the night of the fire.

"I'll be fine," Mama insisted. "I'll get what we need and come right back."

She didn't look that sure of herself. She clasped and unclasped her hands and her face had gone pale, as if she was on the verge of a headache. But no matter what I said, I couldn't convince her to let me go instead. "Just make sure you don't talk to anyone," I finally said.

"I won't."

"And make sure you have your identity document with you."

Mama rummaged in her purse and brought out the paper with her new name—Daria Melnik—written on it. "It's right here in case I'm stopped. But I'm sure I won't be." A brief smile passed over her lips. It felt as if our roles were reversed and Mama knew it. There I was, instructing her to be careful while she was the one assuring me that she would be fine. It was as if I had become the mother and she, the child.

"Please don't worry," she said, looking directly at me. I gave her one long hug before she finally went out the door.

Over the next couple of hours, in between running to get tea for Nina, playing with Nadia, and trying to keep the baby as quiet as possible, I waited by the window, scanning up and down the road and hoping desperately to catch a glimpse of Mama returning home.

By early afternoon, I was beside myself with worry. "It shouldn't have taken her this long," I cried to Nina. She was still in bed, the blankets pulled up to her chin even though the apartment was stiflingly hot. Proskurov was in the middle of a September heat wave. The soaring temperatures outside had invaded our inside space. Sweat dripped down Nina's face. Even her scarf was wet and stained with perspiration. My hair clung to my cheeks in wet ringlets. I had stripped the baby down to her diaper. And Nadia played listlessly with a few of her buttons, rearranging them in the order of when she had found them. Meanwhile, my stomach was in knots waiting for the door to click open and Mama to walk in.

"I'm sure she's fine," Nina said weakly. "Perhaps the tram was slow, or there was a bigger crowd at the market and she had to wait in line. Please try not to worry."

That was what Mama had said before going out the door. But I could tell from Nina's crinkled brow that she was just as nervous as I was. And when another hour had passed with no sign of Mama, I knew there was only one thing to do. I had to go and look for her.

When I told Nina that I was going out, she pushed herself up on one arm from her bed. "No, let me go," she insisted. "If something's happened to your mother, then it may be too dangerous for you to be outside as well."

Nina pulled back her covers, brought one foot down to the floor, and then the other. But when she stood, she swayed and teetered like Galya had when she took her first steps. I grabbed her arms and gently pushed her back onto the bed.

"You can't go out like this, Nina," I said. "You'll pass out on the streets. And especially now, with the heat—it's just too dangerous for you."

"Nonsense," Nina said. She tried to stand once more and then fell heavily onto her bed and leaned back against her pillow. "I can't let you go," she said, breathlessly. "What if someone you know sees you."

She was right about that. The market was the place I had passed every day on my way to school. Mrs. Timko's candy store was right around the corner. Many vendors knew me. The chance of being recognized was high, and that scared me more than I was willing to say. And if Mama had encountered trouble on her trip to the market, what made me think I wouldn't also meet up with danger?

But my need to find her pushed all other thoughts of risk into the background. What if she had hurt herself? What if she was sick? What if she had been arrested? I shoved that last alarming notion as far back as I could.

"I'll take my papers with me in case I'm stopped."

Wasn't that the last thing Mama had also said? "I'll be fine, Nina," I added. "And I'll be back as soon as I can."

Nina reached over to open the small purse that lay next to her. "Here," she said, pulling out some coins. "You'll need this for the tram. And take extra to buy some food if you can."

At first, I didn't want to take the money for food. Mama had gone to buy food, and taking that money from Nina meant that Mama might not be coming back. I couldn't think that—couldn't allow my mind to go there. But Nina was insistent, pushing the money into my hand before finally falling back onto her pillow, too weak to do anything more. Then, she just closed her eyes.

When I stepped outside, the heat nearly swallowed me up. The air was heavy and sticky, with no whisper of a breeze. And the pavement practically shimmered as waves of hot air rose and disappeared upward. Mrs. Sirko was standing in front of the apartment building, fanning herself with a newspaper. She glanced at me as I walked past. Thankfully, she didn't say a word.

Despite the heat, I walked quickly, my head down, eyes on the road in front of me. I figured the less I looked up and around, the less likely it would be that others would notice me. At one point, I practically ran headlong into a woman pushing a baby carriage.

"Watch where you're going," she ordered.

"I'm sorry," I muttered before lowering my head once more and continuing on my way.

The tram was already at the corner. Nina had instructed me on how to board, who to pay, and what to do. The last time I had ridden the tram, Mama had taken care of everything. All I had to do was sit and lean my head out the window. This time, I reached into my pocket, removed the coins Nina had given me, and counted out the exact change that I needed. I felt my heart race as I joined the line of people waiting to board.

"Make room for those getting on," the driver called out to the passengers already inside.

I could see riders inside the tram moving to the back to make space for us. Finally, it was my turn to climb on. Mustering all of my courage, I placed one foot on the step, grabbed the pole, and hoisted myself onto the tram.

"Kamenetsky Street," I said to the driver as I placed the change into his hand. He deposited the money into a silver coin belt that he wore around his waist, with slots for each denomination, and motioned me with his hand to move on in. I breathed a quick sigh of relief as everyone else crowded in after me. The driver rang a bell, and a moment later, the car pitched forward.

A little girl sat with her mother, staring up at me as I made my way toward the back. Her mother held her hand and occasionally reached up to wipe a strand of hair from her face. Then she leaned down to whisper something in the little girl's ear. She laughed and laid her head on her mother's arm. I tried not to stare as thoughts of Mama pounded in my brain. I so desperately wanted her with me, wanted to link my arm with hers, wanted to rest my head against her shoulder. I had to find her. There was no other possibility.

The ride to the center of the city took another ten minutes. The tram stopped several times, and more and more people crammed themselves in until it felt as if the tram would collapse if one more person tried to get on board. Finally, the driver bellowed, "Kamenetsky Street," and brought the tram to a lurching stop. I joined the flood of passengers who poured out onto the street. People pushed past me, eager to get to the market and join the lines that snaked away from just about every vendor's stall and every shop. The little girl and her mother disappeared into the crowd.

As I looked around, fear settled into my stomach once again. How was I ever going to find Mama in this hoard of people? I didn't know where to begin to look. I didn't know how I was going to navigate myself around the shops and stalls. I couldn't ask any questions about Mama—that would arouse suspicion. I knew I had to avoid any shops where I might be recognized. I knew I had to skirt around the groups of soldiers that patrolled here and there. And I knew I had to steer clear of the district to the left of the market, knowing that was where the Jewish ghetto had been set up.

My eyes darted everywhere, searching the crowd, searching the streets. Nothing! All the while, I continued to pray that Mama would just appear in front of me. She'd smile and explain that the shopping had taken her longer than she had planned. She had lost track of time. Then she'd grab me in a big hug and we'd head back home. But even as I wished that would happen, I felt in my heart that it wouldn't. My stomach sank further and further into a deep pit of gloom.

I finally joined a line in front of a stall selling bread. As much as I didn't want to admit that Mama was in danger, I knew that Nina was right: we needed food. And standing in line gave me another chance to scan the market area for Mama. Still nothing!

Eventually, I reached the front of the line and bought my bread. What to do next? Where to look? I had been here for nearly an hour, and Nina would be beside herself with worry. Should I go home? Should I stay and search? Those competing choices battled in my brain as I stood frozen in the middle of the street.

And then, someone called my name.

CHAPTER 23

"Eldina?"

It was a man's voice, and it came from right behind me. I froze, my heart beginning to pound.

"Eldina? Is that you?"

I didn't recognize the voice and had no idea who was standing behind me, but every nerve in my body was on guard for trouble. All I wanted to do was run—far and fast. Perhaps I could vanish into the crowd or hide behind a stall and not be seen. I wished I could sprout wings and fly into the air and back to the safety of the apartment. But even as I thought desperately of ways to disappear, I knew it wasn't possible. Running would only draw more attention to me.

"Eldina!"

The voice behind me was more persistent as the

man called my name for a third time. I took a deep breath, turned ever so slowly, and looked up and into the face of my old school teacher, Mr. Petrenko.

If my heart had been beating quickly before, it now began to gallop at full speed. This was my nightmare come true. My teacher! My mind instantly flashed back to the time he had refused to step in when Avrum was being bullied, and the time he had moved me and all the Jewish students to the back of the classroom. My teacher had not been a friend or a helper. And he knew me. He knew I was Jewish.

Mr. Petrenko stepped closer to me, swinging his lame leg forward, and I backed away, my eyes searching in all directions for a clear path of escape. I knew I could outrun him because of his bad leg, but he could yell at others to catch me, which would be even worse. But what could I say to him? How could I explain being here in the market, and not wearing a Star of David badge on my clothes? How could I explain not being inside the ghetto where all Jews were supposed to go? Even now, Mr. Petrenko's eyes moved to my blouse and to the spot where the star should have been. Instinctively, I reached up to cover my shirt, while the pounding in my chest moved up to my ears. I thought my head was going to explode.

We stood there, staring at one another. And then,

Mr. Petrenko put his hand, gently, on my arm.

"Come with me," he said softly. "Don't say a word."

With his arm linked through mine, Mr. Petrenko began to steer me through the crowd, his leg swinging in a furious semicircle. At first, I yanked back, trying to resist his pull.

"Please!" Mr. Petrenko said, tightening his hold on my arm. "I'm not going to hurt you."

I didn't believe him: How could I? I was convinced that he was going to lead me to a police station, where he would turn me over to the authorities. I would end up in the ghetto or in some terrible prison far away and never see my family again. But I knew I had no choice but to allow him to pull me along. I hung my head, defeated, like a prisoner walking to the gallows.

No one seemed to take notice as we walked past vendor stalls and shops. We rounded a corner and began to leave the market area. The further from the market we walked, the more terrified I became. It was only when we finally came to a stop that I dared to look up. Rather than faing a police station, though, we were standing in front of a small café. Still holding my arm, Mr. Petrenko guided me through the door and led me to a table at the back of the shop. Gently but firmly, he pushed me into a chair and took a seat across from me. I couldn't look at him. My eyes were lowered, staring at a stain on the blue tablecloth. I was still terrified, and I still didn't know what was going on or why he had brought me here. Mr. Petrenko ordered tea, and we sat in silence until the tea had been placed before us.

"Have something to drink," he finally said.

Head still down, I reached for my teacup, bringing it to my lips with hands that shook uncontrollably. The hot liquid scalded my tongue as I took a big sip. But the pain barely registered.

"Eldina," he said. "Please look at me."

That's when I finally raised my head and stared into his eyes. What I saw took me aback. There was no anger there, no hatred. He didn't look as if he was out to get me. What I saw was genuine concern.

"I'm not going to hurt you," Mr. Petrenko said again. "Please believe me. I just thought it was best to get you off the street."

I nodded, still unable to say a word.

"What were you doing out there? And all by yourself!" He glanced again at the shoulder of my blouse, where the star should have been stitched. "Don't you know how dangerous this is for you? Where's your mother?"

With that question, tears began to stream down my cheeks—tears that I'd been holding in since

Mama had left for the market earlier that day. I hung my head and wept, taking in gulps of air between sobs.

Mr. Petrenko didn't say a word. At one point, he passed me a handkerchief, which I held up to my face. I continued to cry until there were no more tears left. And then I just sat, sniffling and hiccupping while my shoulders shook and heaved. And then I looked up.

"I'm sorry," I murmured.

"Do you think you could tell me what's happened?" Mr. Petrenko asked. "Please," he added. "I'd like to help."

I stared at my former teacher, needing to believe that he did indeed want to help. And then, I took a deep breath and began to explain everything—the fire, our lost papers, my uncle and his stony-faced wife, the county official and how Nina had gotten us new names and new identity documents and a new place to live. Finally, I told him about Mama going to the market and not coming home. A couple of times, Mr. Petrenko asked some questions: how long Mama had been gone, who might have seen her, which stalls she might have gone to, who she might have spoken to. I answered them as best I could. At one point, he signaled the café owner to bring us more tea, along with a sandwich for me. I gulped it down, suddenly aware that I was famished; I hadn't eaten for hours. I talked for a long time. And I realized as I confessed my story that Mr. Petrenko really did care. He had already had a couple of chances to turn me in, but he hadn't. I knew I could trust him, and it felt good to tell him everything.

"I need to find my mother," I finally whispered, before slumping in my seat and lowering my head once more. A long time passed in silence. When I finally looked up, Mr. Petrenko was still staring at me. Suddenly, he rose from the table.

"I have a friend," he said, somewhat urgently. "He's connected to the authorities. But he's a good man," he added, noting the sudden alarm in my eyes. "I want you to wait here. I'm going to try to find out what I can."

And then he was gone—out the door of the café and heading back in the direction of the market, leg swinging rapidly as he walked. The owner of the café stared at me briefly and then went back to serving his other customers. I lowered my head on the tablecloth once more and closed my eyes. I was exhausted. The strain of worrying about Mama, the shock of seeing Mr. Petrenko, everything that had happened to my family—it all came crashing down on me. Suddenly, all I wanted to do was go to sleep and wake up with

Mama back in our home and everything back to normal—or at least the normal that we had created in the last few weeks. For that, I would do anything.

I don't know how long I sat there. I must have dozed off. The next thing I knew, someone was shaking me gently on the shoulder. When I looked up, Mr. Petrenko was standing over me. He sank heavily into his seat across from me. His face was gray and I braced myself.

Mr. Petrenko shook his head. "It's not good news," he said. "I'm afraid that she's been arrested."

Despite the oppressive heat, an icy chill passed over me. I shuddered.

"Someone must have seen her," he continued. "Someone who knew who she was and reported it."

My mouth was dry. "Where is she?" I croaked out the question.

"My friend tells me she's been taken to the ghetto."

I was feeling light-headed. Mr. Petrenko's face swam before my eyes. I lowered my head once more and bit my lip, trying to steady myself and focus on what my teacher was saying.

"Look at me, Eldina," Mr. Petrenko urged. I looked up and he said, "The good news is that she's safe."

Safe! She was locked away in some prison that

sounded terrible. That didn't sound safe to me. "Can I see her?" I asked.

He shook his head. "I'm afraid not. And it's best if you don't go anywhere near the ghetto."

"But—"

He held up his hand to stop me. "I'll ask my friend to get a message to her, letting her know that you are aware of what's happened to her. That's the best I can do."

I nodded—numb and completely worn out. When I glanced out the window, I could see that the sun was starting to go down. Where had this day gone? Nina would be frantic with worry.

"Go home, Eldina," Mr. Petrenko continued. "You're lucky that your housekeeper is willing to protect you. Others have not been so lucky."

I nodded again. In that moment, I didn't feel particularly lucky. I looked over at Mr. Petrenko. "Thank you," I whispered. "Thank you for helping me. I thought when I saw you ..." I didn't finish the sentence.

"These are terrible times," Mr. Petrenko said. "I want you to know that I wish circumstances were different. And I wish there was more I could do to help."

With that, I finally rose from the table. Before leaving the café, Mr. Petrenko stopped me one more time. "I wish you good luck, Eldina. You and your family."

I left the café as the sun was disappearing below the horizon. And then I ran for the tram to take me home.

CHAPTER 24

Nina was pacing the kitchen floor when I flew in the door and threw myself into her arms, practically pushing her over.

"Dina!" she cried, holding me tightly and stroking my head. "I was scared to death that something had happened to you."

At first, I couldn't talk—I was shaking so badly in Nina's arms.

"Where have you been? Are you all right? Tell me what happened!" Nina sounded as terrified as I was feeling. When I finally looked at her, her face was still pale. I couldn't tell if it was from having been sick earlier in the day or because of her worry for me.

"I'm okay," I stammered. And then, standing right there in the kitchen, I poured out the whole story to her—going to the market, searching everywhere, seeing Mr. Petrenko, his information about Mama. "He said that she's been arrested. She's in the ghetto."

Nina sucked in her breath and her eyes grew wide.

"What are we going to do?" I asked.

Nadia was hovering in the background, listening in on the conversation. "Is Mama okay?" she asked.

Nina and I glanced at one another. How could I explain to Nadia what was going on? I barely understood it myself. And what could I say that wouldn't scare her? I was scared enough for the two of us.

"We're not sure, Nadia," I began.

"I know what the ghetto is." Nadia's face was unsmiling. "I heard you and Mama talking about it one night. You thought I was sleeping, but I wasn't. I heard what you said."

I stared at Nadia, still unsure how to respond.

"I pretended that Nina was our mother when we went to that building and that man was asking all those questions," Nadia continued. "I can keep a secret about anything."

"I know you can. But I don't know what more I can tell you."

"Will Mama be coming home soon?" She stared up at me, eyes trusting and hopeful.

I shook my head. "I don't think so."

"Do you think she's scared?"

"Probably a little bit," I replied, my voice catching in my throat. "But Mama's strong. And I know she wants us to be strong as well."

That's when Nina took Nadia's hands. "Yes," she said. "We all need to be strong for each other. Now," Nina continued, "let's sit down together—as a family—and talk about what we're going to do to find out more about your mama."

We spent the next hours trying to figure out a plan. Nina suggested we go to my uncle. He had told us to stay in touch, even if the offer was half-hearted. Still, I couldn't risk exposing him. He was in the same situation as we were. He was Jewish too and trying to hide it. I thought about going to seek out Mr. Petrenko again. Maybe his friend could give us more information. But it would be impossible to find my teacher a second time. And he had been so unexpectedly kind to me that I didn't want to put him in any more danger. He had already risked a lot by getting me the information about Mama's arrest.

We talked in circles about the possibilities. Every idea we turned over seemed to result in a dead end except for one that we kept coming back to. It was the only option we had. We needed to go to the ghetto ourselves and see if we could find Mama. I didn't know what we'd do after we found her; we didn't even talk about that. But at the very least, I needed to see her and make sure she was okay.

At first, Nina wanted to go on her own. "It won't matter if someone I know sees me. I can be on the streets and there's no danger."

I knew that was true. But I desperately wanted to go with her. "I have to see Mama for myself," I said. "I'll keep my head down," I added, echoing Mama's words.

"I don't know," Nina began.

"Please," I begged. "I need to see her."

We talked back and forth for a few more minutes. And then Nina nodded.

"All right," she said. She didn't look convinced. "We'll go first thing tomorrow morning. But you will stay by my side the whole time. Is that clear?"

"Of course!" I practically shouted at her.

"What about me?" Nadia pulled on my arm and I turned to face her. "Can I come?" she asked. "I want to see Mama too." Her solemn expression nearly broke my heart.

I stared into Nadia's serious eyes. A part of me really wanted to take her along, knowing how much she wanted to be with Mama. But I couldn't chance putting her and the baby in danger. Finally, I knelt down before my little sister and took her hands. "It's just not safe for all of us to go out together. Besides," I added as Nadia's face fell, "you have a very big job to do while we're away, Nadia. Someone has to look after Galya. You know we can't take her with us. You've never done that before. Do you think you can do it now?"

Galya was waddling around the kitchen table, holding a small blanket up to her face. When she heard me mention her, she paused, turned, and gave me the biggest, most joyful smile. Nadia stared at Galya and then pulled her shoulders back and nodded. "I can do it," she declared. I reached over and enfolded her in a big hug.

The next morning, just as Nina and I were preparing to leave the apartment, Nadia came over to me one more time. "If you see Mama, will you hug her for me? Will you tell her I'm looking after the baby like a big girl?"

I could have cried. I stared down at my little sister, knowing she had one foot still in childhood and one in the adult nightmare of prisons and arrests. It was so unfair that she had to live like that. It was unfair for all of us. "I'll tell her, Nadia," I said. "She'll be so proud of you."

Nadia beamed, and Nina and I set off.

Mrs. Sirko was in front of the apartment when we left the building.

"Good morning, Mrs. Sirko," Nina said politely. She had also introduced herself to our neighbor on one of the occasions when she'd gone to the market to shop for us.

The neighbor glanced at her but turned to me instead. "My, my," she said. "You seem to be very busy lately—going in and out. Where are you off to today?"

I paused and smiled faintly. I felt as if I had to give this woman something or she would be too suspicious. "My mother and I are spending the day together," I said, linking arms with Nina as we walked away. I could almost feel our neighbor staring after us.

We caught the tram to the center of the city. Then we walked past the market where vendors were starting to unpack their belongings and set up their displays for the day. Early shoppers were already starting to form lines, eager to be the first to buy from an ever-dwindling supply of food. I stayed as close to Nina as I could, holding her arm and keeping my head down. My stomach was flip-flopping and my heart was pounding like thunder the whole time we walked. I was terrified that someone would spot me— someone who didn't have the good intentions of Mr. Petrenko. Luckily, no one seemed to be paying attention to the woman with the scarf on her head or the young girl hanging on to her. Nina had chosen to wear the gray scarf that my uncle's wife had given her. It made her look less obvious, she had said. We passed by the market unnoticed and turned the corner off Kamenetsky Street toward the place where the ghetto had been set up. Up ahead, I could see a tall wooden gate I'd never seen before. Stretching away from it on either side were rows of wire with jagged barbs sticking out. Further down the road and on either side of the gate, men were hammering stumps of wood into the ground and running more rows of barbed wire between the poles. Dozens of soldiers, with guns at the ready, patrolled along the wire fence.

And through the wires, I could see hundreds and hundreds of people shuffling along the road on the other side, holding on to their family members—wives, husbands, grandparents, children. I recognized Mr. Rabinovich, the tailor who had retired years earlier, and Mrs. Levich who sold cheese in the marketplace, along with other familiar faces. These were the Jewish citizens of Proskurov—my community—all imprisoned behind wire bars, caged as if they were dangerous animals. All around me, other citizens of Proskurov walked past the ghetto, staring at the Jews inside as if they were exhibits in a zoo, pausing every now and then to point and whisper to one an-other. Periodically, the soldiers ordered these people to move on.

It took all of my control not to burst into tears. I was breathing quickly and holding on to Nina with all my might. "Stay calm," Nina whispered to me.

Somewhere in there was Mama. I had to find her. "Let's get closer," I whispered back.

We moved toward the wire, careful to time our approach to when the soldiers had passed and were patrolling further down. I began to scan the faces of those inside. Everyone looked miserable and hope-lessly sad. Their heads were downturned. Their steps were slow. Children cried. Elderly men and women looked terrified. I bit my lower lip, steeling myself to the pain I could see, and continued to search for my mother. And then, suddenly, I spotted a woman sit-ting on the curb inside the wire prison. She hugged her knees tight to her chest and rested her head on her legs. I didn't have to see her face to know that it was Mama.

I nearly shouted out loud. Only Nina's firm grasp of my arm stopped me. And then, as if she sensed my presence, Mama looked up. Her face lit up when she saw me. Quickly and soundlessly, she stood from her spot and moved close to the wire where Nina and I

were standing. I glanced in both directions as she approached. The soldiers were out of sight, still patrolling further down the road. Mama stepped nearer.

"You mustn't be here," she warned, speaking almost without moving her lips.

"Mama!" I didn't know what else to say. She was
so close I could have almost reached out and touched
her hand. I wanted to so desperately, but I didn't dare.

"I'm okay—really I am." She looked as if she wanted to reach out to me as well. "How are Nadia and the
baby?"

"They're fine. We're all fine. We couldn't bring
them," I added.

Mama nodded. "Hug them for me. Tell them I
love them."

"We've been so worried about you," Nina said.

Mama glanced at her and then back at me. "And
I've been worried about you too. Someone told me
that you knew about my arrest."

I quickly told her about Mr. Petrenko and his
friend who had helped get her that information.

"I was relieved to hear that you knew. But it's
much too dangerous for you to be here!"

"What happened, Mama?" I croaked out. "How
did you get arrested?" It was taking all of my strength
to stop myself from crying. Seeing Mama behind

these wire bars was almost too much to bear.

Mama sighed. "I ran into Mrs. Timko in the market." She almost spat the name out. "As soon as she saw me, she started shouting for the police. I showed them my papers—tried to convince them that I didn't know what she was talking about, but it was no use."

Mrs. Timko! The candy lady! The woman with the forever smile and sweets for everyone had turned out to be more treacherous than anyone.

"I'm not hurt," Mama said, noting the look of distress on my face. "But most importantly, you are all safe."

"But what are we going to do?" I glanced up and down the wire again. I knew we only had seconds before the guards might return.

Mama shook her head. "There's nothing we can do." And before I could protest, she turned to Nina. "Go home. Don't come back here, Nina. Please, keep my children safe."

Nina nodded and pulled me close to her. "I will. They're my family too." Then she reached into her purse and pulled out some money, quickly pushing the bills through the wire and into Mama's hands. "You'll need this—for food, or bribes, or something."

Mama nodded gratefully and shoved the money into her pocket. Then she looked at me once more.

"Remember that I love you very much—you and your sisters. And I'm always watching over you, no matter what. Will you remember that?" Mama was starting to cry, and the tears were flowing down my cheeks as well.

"I'll remember."

"Stay safe for me," she said. Then she blew me a kiss and turned away from the wire just as a soldier came close.

"Move on," he ordered.

Just before stepping back, I caught a glimpse of one more familiar sight inside the wire prison— something appearing and disappearing into the mass of sad people shuffling by—color in a sea of gray. It was red—faded and dirty—but I knew instantly what it was. Esther's red coat! And when I looked more carefully, I could see my friend, wearing her favorite coat despite the oppressive heat, and following behind her parents and brother on the other side of the barbed-wire fence. I froze. Nina followed my gaze and gasped out loud. But Esther didn't look my way, and I couldn't call out to her. What would I have said? And how could I have explained my freedom when she was imprisoned like this?

It was more than I could take. With a heart that felt as if it were breaking, I turned and walked away from the ghetto, my arm linked tight with Nina's. I didn't look back. Neither of us said a word the whole way home.

CHAPTER 25

Nina wouldn't let us out of the apartment after that—not for air, not to go for a walk, not to play on the steps, not for anything. It reminded me of when we had barred ourselves indoors before the fire had consumed our house. But this time was so much worse. This time, Mama wasn't with us.

I couldn't bear to think of my mother, though at times I couldn't stop myself. I pictured her alone, walking the streets of the ghetto. Did she have enough to eat? Did she have a place to sleep? Was she warm enough, now that the days and nights were beginning to cool down? Was she getting sick? My heart was heavier than ever. And just when I thought I couldn't feel any sadder, I would picture Esther, following her parents and brother, wearing her faded red coat, and all the same worries about *her* safety would come crashing down on me.

I hadn't said much to Nadia about having seen Mama. It was hard to answer all of the questions my little sister had.

"Did you give her a hug for me?"

"I couldn't really hug her, but I told her that you sent her all your love."

"Did you tell her I was looking after the baby like a big girl?"

"Of course. And she was so proud of you."

"Did she look sad?"

That one nearly brought me to my knees. "She's really glad that we're all safe."

That seemed to satisfy Nadia, and she retreated to her corner of the sitting room.

Nina continued to shop in the market, though less often. She didn't want to leave us alone. I practically pounced on her the minute she returned from her excursions, overwhelming her with questions in the same way Nadia had bombarded me. Nina had few answers.

"Did you go by the ghetto? Did you see Mama? Did you hear any news?"

She always just shook her head. "It's impossible to get close to that place now. Soldiers are everywhere. But, I'm here for you, always," she would add. "I'll do whatever I have to do to keep you safe."

I wanted to smile when she said that—just to show her how grateful I was. But I couldn't. I felt gloomy and without hope.

And when we listened to the news on the radio, it was clear that things were getting worse all the time. Sometimes, Nina suggested that we turn the radio off. "It doesn't help to listen to such terrible reports," she said.

But as scary as things sounded, I felt I needed to know what was happening. It was clear that, between Hitler's Germany on one side and Stalin's Soviet Russia on the other, my country was a pawn, caught in the middle of a war over land and power, and it was being destroyed. And neither the Germans nor the Russians wanted the Jews. Nearly every day, there were reports of Jews being shot on the streets of Proskurov, mostly those who hadn't reported to the ghetto and had been discovered hiding with kind families or in deserted buildings in and around the city. Whenever a report like that was broadcast, Nina leapt to her feet and quickly turned the radio off.

Every day, I tried to make myself believe that we were safe where we were, and that Mama, though imprisoned in the ghetto, was safe as well. Each night, before going to sleep, I pulled the Star of David necklace from under my pillow and fastened it around my neck. And then, I whispered a prayer to Mama. "I won't forget you, or Papa. I pray we'll see each other soon. And even though we're here with Nina pretending that she's our mother, I know who my real parents are. And I'll never forget that either."

Over the next few weeks, with Mama gone and with nothing to do all day, we settled into a strange routine. Nadia continued to play with her button collection, though it had stopped growing, as if frozen in time. The baby played, but more quietly now, hardly giggling or cooing anymore.

As for me, I got used to doing nothing, staying indoors—something I never would have thought possible six months ago. I daydreamed about happier times with no one to stop me. Sometimes, I even dared to imagine being reunited with Mama—running into her arms and telling her everything that had happened since she'd been arrested. I pictured her enfolding me into a big hug. And then she and I would sit at the kitchen table, one of us would make tea, and we'd talk for hours. Those daydreams were the best moments of all.

I was having just such a daydream, sitting at the kitchen table with Nina and my sisters, when someone pounded on the door. We all froze. I locked eyes with Nina, whose face was ashen.

"Who do you think it is?" I whispered.

Nina shook her head and put her finger across her lips to tell me to stay quiet. I nodded, hoping that whoever was there would give up and leave. But a moment later, the pounding resumed, followed by a man's harsh voice that seemed to fill our apartment.

"Open up. We need to search this place."

Nina's face was whiter than I had ever seen. Nadia sat staring straight ahead. The baby had gone quiet and still, her eyes wide and startled. My heart began to pound out of my chest, rising up to fill my ears—thumping, thumping.

There was another loud rap at the door and an angry shout from outside. "Open up, now!"

Nina looked at all of us. "Let me do the talking," she said under her breath as she rose from the table, wrapped her shawl around her shoulders, took a deep breath, and walked over to unlock the door. Three soldiers in gray uniforms with thick black belts and high leather boots pushed the door open and shoved past Nina. They filled the apartment like dark clouds. I stood from the table, pulling Nadia along with me to a corner of the room.

I had read enough newspaper accounts and heard

enough radio reports to know instantly that they were part of the Gestapo—the secret police of Nazi Germany. Their job was to round up Jews from across Europe and send them to those terrifying prisons. One soldier walked into the bedroom, another into the kitchen. The tallest of the three began to talk.

"Your name, madame?" he asked Nina.

"Ludviga Pukas." Her voice was remarkably calm.

The officer pointed to me and my sisters. "And who are they?"

"My daughters," Nina replied with no hesitation.

"Their names?"

"Eldina, Gennadiy, and Galya." Nina swept the baby into her arms as she spoke. Galya was still silent, her body stiff in Nina's arms.

The officer barely acknowledged us. "Papers," he demanded, holding out his hand with a beckoning motion.

Nina went to her purse and pulled out our identity documents. It was only then that I could see how her hands were shaking. Instinctively, I pulled Nadia closer to me as Nina handed the papers over to the Gestapo.

"May I ask what this is about?" she asked.

At first, the officer didn't reply. He took the papers and began to inspect them. Then he looked up.

"We've had a report that you may be harboring a Jew here." He leaned forward to peer at Nina. "You do know that is illegal, don't you?"

My mind began to race. A report? Who had reported us? The nosy neighbor? Mrs. Timko? Someone who had spotted Nina and me near the ghetto?

Nina didn't flinch. "Of course I'm aware of the laws. You can see there is no one here other than me and my children."

I pulled Nadia even closer to me, squeezing her tightly. She flinched under my arm and turned to look up at me. That was when her face froze, her eyes dropping to my chest—to the Star of David that still hung around my neck. My star! I always remembered to remove it in the morning and put it back under my pillow for the day. But this morning I had forgotten. Nadia's eyes widened.

The officer was still talking to Nina. "We'll search for ourselves and see what we can find."

From the bedroom I could hear one officer moving our beds and overturning the contents of our dresser drawers. The one in the kitchen was opening cupboard doors and pulling things from inside, then dumping them on the floor. Nadia was still staring at me, eyes glued to the star that hung around my neck. A trickle of sweat began to roll down my back.

I quickly raised my hand to cover the star. Then I slipped it into my blouse, one eye on the guard who was doing all the talking, praying that he hadn't seen me.

He was still standing in front of Nina, staring at her face and then down at our identity documents. Back and forth his gaze swung—papers, Nina, papers, Nina—like the weighted pendulum inside the old grandfather clock that had sat in our house, the clock that had gone up in flames along with everything else we had owned. I hadn't thought about that clock in such a long time. I stared down at the floor and suddenly noticed a spider creeping across the room, falling into the small ruts and grooves between the planks of wood and then reappearing, regaining its balance, and moving forward again. Silently, I began to root for the spider, hoping it would make its way across the floor and into the safety of the wall on the other side. The Gestapo officer began talking again.

"Is there no one else who lives here?"

He took a step closer to Nina at the exact moment that the spider veered and walked into his path. The soldier lifted his foot. The spider moved under it. I gasped out loud and the soldier turned his head to look at me. I glanced up at him and then lowered my eyes as he swung around and approached.

"What was your name again?" he asked, stopping inches from me and bending forward, his dark piercing eyes staring menacingly into mine. His neck was as thick as a tree trunk and his belly threatened to pop through the buttons of his jacket.

I could almost feel my star pressing against my chest under my blouse. Would he notice? "My mother already told you," I said, somehow finding my voice. "I'm Eldina Pukas."

He looked at our documents, shuffling the pages to find mine. "Yes, Eldina," he said. Then he looked back at me. "Is there no one else who lives here? You can tell me." He leaned down until I could feel his breath across my face. I cringed and felt a shudder go through Nadia.

"No!" I stammered, nearly gagging from the smell of eggs mixed with cigarette smoke that wafted from his mouth. "There's no one else."

That was when Nina stepped in again, positioning herself between the officer and us.

"I had a housekeeper," she said, pulling the soldier's gaze away from me. "But she left us."

The officer paused. "A housekeeper?"

"Yes," Nina replied, shifting the baby to her other arm. "With my meager savings, it was impossible to pay her any longer."

"And where did this … housekeeper go?" he asked.

I thought about Mama and held my breath.

Nina pulled herself up as tall as she could. "I'm afraid I have no idea."

The officer paused again. He stared once more at our documents. Finally, he snapped his fingers and called for his colleagues to join him. Then he handed our identity papers back to Nina and clicked his heels together.

"That's all … for now," he added.

With that, the three Gestapo officials turned and walked out the door. I glanced down at the floor just in time to see the spider make it safely to the other side of the room. It disappeared behind a floorboard as our door closed with a loud thud.

CHAPTER 26

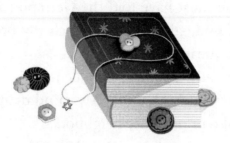

At first, no one moved. I stayed glued to my spot, my arm firmly encircling Nadia, trying to regain the breath I had lost during that encounter with the Gestapo. My head was still spinning and I felt faint. The sight of that officer's face so close to mine—his foul breath pouring over me—it was almost too much.

Without talking, the three of us eventually stumbled to the kitchen table. Nadia and I fell into our chairs. Nina placed the baby back into her high chair, her arms shaking, and then sat heavily next to us. Galya was still quiet, eyes wide, watching each one of us as if she needed to know that everything was okay. I reached over and stroked her cheek, tickling her behind her ear until I felt her relax and she began to giggle softly again. Then I put my arm around Nadia's shoulders, which felt stiff and knotted. I finally looked over at Nina. The color was beginning to come back into her cheeks.

"Someone must have told the Gestapo something about us," I said, still trying to catch my breath and slow my heartbeat.

Nina nodded. "Yes, that must be true."

"Who do you think told?" My mind drifted again to Mrs. Timko or our nosy neighbor.

"It doesn't matter," Nina replied. "The important thing is that I think we fooled them."

I still wasn't convinced. "Do you think they'll be back?"

Nina hesitated a second and then she said, "I hope not. But if they do, we'll be prepared." She reached out and grabbed my hand and then Nadia's. She held both our hands in hers. "You darling girls," she said, her voice catching. "You were both so brave."

Nadia smiled faintly, and then lowered her head onto the table as if it was too heavy to hold up any longer.

"You too, Nina," I said. "I can't believe how calm you sounded. And the way you answered that soldier—I don't know what we would have done without you."

Nina took the three of us in with her sweeping

gaze, and then stood up from the table. "Come, girls," she said firmly. "Help me clean up the mess in the kitchen. I want to wash every single dish we have—anything that those evil men may have touched."

"I'll clean up the bedroom," I said, also rising and moving toward my room. When I walked in, I gasped out loud. It looked as if a hurricane had hit. The mattresses were upturned; sheets had been pulled from the beds and tossed aside. Our clothing was piled in a heap in the middle of the floor. Nadia's button collection was scattered everywhere. My heart sank once more as I stared at the mess. And that was when I noticed my pillow. It was on the floor, a boot print clearly visible in the middle of it.

I shrieked out loud. That brought Nadia and Nina running.

"What? What is it?" Nina cried. Her face had gone pale again.

I pointed at the floor and at my pillow. But at first, Nina didn't understand. She reached over to hug me. "It's okay," she said. "I'll wash all the sheets and the pillowcases. As soon as we're finished in the kitchen, we'll all help clean up in here. You don't have to—"

"No," I cried, pulling away from her. "You don't understand." And then I reached up to pull my Star of David necklace from inside my blouse. I grasped the star in between my fingers and held it up to Nina. "I wore this today. I forgot to take it off. I was wearing it when the soldiers were searching the apartment."

Nina stared at the star and gasped as she finally understood what I was trying to say. Had I remembered to take my necklace off and place it under my pillow, the Gestapo would have surely found it. And who knew what might have happened to us then! The shocking reality set in that by wearing the star, I had prevented us from being discovered.

"What made you keep it on, today of all days?" Nina asked.

I shook my head. "It was an accident. But a good one," I quickly added.

"It was Mama," Nadia said solemnly.

"What do you mean?" I asked.

"Mama," she repeated. "She must have been looking out for us."

Mama! Had this been a sign from her? Had her voice been in my head when I dressed in the morning, whispering to me to keep the star on? She had said that she would always be watching over us—protecting us whether or not she was by our side. Maybe, just maybe, she was the one who had helped save us today.

I nodded and smiled, believing in my heart that

this was indeed true. "I think you may be right, Nadia."

Then I pressed the star to my lips, took a deep breath, and with Nadia and Nina by my side, we began to clean up.

EPILOGUE

Four Years Later

"Are you ready?" Nina asked from the doorway of my room.

I sighed as I looked into the mirror and brushed my long blond hair into a tight ponytail at the back of my head. "No, but I guess I have no choice."

"They're just trying to do what they think is right." Nina walked into the room and came to stand beside me. She looked into the mirror and adjusted the scarf around her head. Since the war had ended a year earlier, she had taken to wearing patterned scarves. They were just as colorful as before, and today, she wore one that had yellow daisies against a bright green background.

I ignored her comment. "Where's Nadia?" I asked instead.

"She's already in the sitting room with them."

"And Galya?" At five years of age, my little sister was no longer a baby, and I couldn't refer to her as one.

"She's there as well." Nina paused and then added, "Just try to be patient with them."

I sighed with irritation. It was exactly what Mama had said to me the first time I'd met Nina—so many years ago, when things had seemed so much simpler. But this was a different time, and I wasn't sure I could be patient with the people waiting for me out in the sitting room.

I turned to face Nina. "Just give me another minute."

She nodded, and then left the room. I turned back to the mirror and looked at myself. My face was as serious as it always was—maybe even more so after everything my family had been through. Mama had always said that I looked older than my years. I pinched my pale cheeks to bring some color into them and finally reached into my blouse to pull my Star of David necklace out.

We had managed to live out the rest of the war in this apartment, keeping our heads down, as Mama had always instructed, and staying away from any trouble. Nadia and I had even gone back to school— one that was far from our old neighborhood and far from anyone who might have known us. There, we continued to hide our Jewish faith, mixing in with all the Catholic children. Luckily, the Gestapo never returned to search our apartment.

When the war ended, we began to look for Mama. We searched everywhere. We had heard the news reports—all the Jews imprisoned in the Proskurov ghetto had been taken outside the city and shot. But we didn't want to believe it. So we spoke with dozens of people—those who lived close to the ghetto, those who knew of people who had been imprisoned there. I even spoke with Mr. Petrenko, who materialized one day on our doorstep, wanting to see how I was. I wasn't sure how he had found us, but I was grateful to see him—finally able to thank him for helping me that day in the market. When he and everyone else confirmed what had happened in the ghetto, we also had to finally accept the truth. It was almost too much to think that Mama had died in that way—all alone and probably scared out of her mind. But there was no other possibility. And Esther and her family had probably died too, along with the thousands of others imprisoned there. I had cried for weeks before finally accepting this news. Every last particle of hope had evaporated. I spent days lying in my bed, curled into a tight ball, not wanting to talk to anyone.

I wanted to crawl into a hole and never come out. I felt empty, like my insides had been scooped out, the way we dug the seeds out of a melon. Thank goodness Nina had been there—always there—to sit with me and hold me until I was ready to face the world again.

And it wasn't only the Jews of Proskurov who had been killed in this terrible and senseless war. Millions and millions of Jews across Europe had died or been killed in horrible conditions that, even now, I found impossibly difficult to imagine. I knew that my sisters and I were among the lucky ones. And for that, we had Nina to thank. She had kept us safe, even though she knew that the penalty for hiding Jews was as bad as being Jewish yourself—imprisonment, torture, death. Nina had ignored all of that and stayed with us. She was and always would be our guardian angel—along with Mama, who I knew watched over me, and even Papa, who I believed had never stopped looking out for me.

I heard someone cough in the room next door, and I knew I couldn't wait any longer. With one last glance in the mirror, I turned and walked into the sitting room. My uncle Leo and his wife, Maria, rose when I entered. Nadia and Galya sat together on the sofa across from them. Nina sat in a chair beside them. I joined my sisters on the sofa.

"Hello, Eldina," my uncle began. "You're looking well. We're relieved to see that."

I gazed at him, startled once more at how much of my father I could see in his face. The war and passage of time had aged him. His hair was gray, his cheeks sagged, and there were deep lines curved around his mouth and at the corners of his eyes. I wondered if that was what Papa would have looked like had he lived.

"We've been worried about you all this time," my uncle continued. "You and your sisters."

I frowned, thinking about the last time I'd seen him. My uncle had been worried, it's true—enough to take us in for a few days, and to give Mama some money when we left. My aunt hadn't wanted anything to do with us. And when I looked at her now, it seemed nothing had changed. She didn't greet me, didn't even look up when I came in; she just sat quietly next to my uncle, her head lowered. What was she thinking? Did she want to be here? Or had my uncle convinced her to come, just as he had convinced her to let us in that dark night years earlier.

My uncle was talking again. "As I was telling your housekeeper—"

"She's Mama," I interrupted.

"Excuse me?"

"Mama," I repeated. "That's what we call her—not our housekeeper."

It was true. We had continued to refer to Nina as our mother even after the war ended. In my heart, I knew she wasn't my mother by blood. But she was the only mother I had now—the only one I'd had for a long time. Nina wasn't saying a word. Her eyes moved across our faces.

"Yes, well," my uncle stammered. "As I was saying to … as I was saying, we feel it's our duty to take you into our home, now that we know that your mother is … isn't … is … isn't coming back."

I could see beads of perspiration dotting his forehead.

"Yes, it's our duty," my aunt said, finally looking up at me and then lowering her eyes once more.

"We've discussed it," my uncle continued. "And we agree. We think you three girls should move in with us."

With that, he sat back in his chair, pulled a handkerchief from his pocket, and wiped his brow. No one spoke for the longest time. We all just sat there staring at one another, except for my aunt, who continued to stare at the floor. I could hear the faucet in the kitchen dripping. It always dripped, no matter what we did to try and stop it. The plunk, plunk, plunk of the water plopping in the sink suddenly reminded me of the old grandfather clock that had sat in our home ticking out the seconds. Mama had said that the sound was like her mother's heartbeat.

"Where have you been?" I suddenly asked, leaning toward my uncle.

He looked startled. "I beg your pardon?"

"All those years that we were hiding here after our mother was arrested, where were you all that time?"

My uncle glanced at his wife and back at me. "I said that you should stay in touch with us. I told your mother that. But you never did."

I frowned again. "How were we supposed to do that when we couldn't even poke our noses out the door? Didn't you think about that? You could have found a way to find us—to help us."

"Dina, please don't be disrespectful," Nina said, a note of warning in her voice.

I took a breath. "I'm not trying to be rude—really, I'm not. But I have to know why you didn't come to us then."

"We were afraid," my uncle said quietly. "Even though Maria is Christian, I didn't know how long my wife's religion would protect me. I thought if I did anything to bring attention to myself, I'd—we'd be targeted too."

I nodded. I understood about keeping your head down—Mama's favorite expression. And I really wasn't angry with my uncle. The truth was that many people—*most* people—had been afraid. "We were scared too," I said.

"You have to understand how dangerous it was for us," my aunt said. "Too dangerous to do anything to help."

My eye widened. "But don't you see," I said, looking over at Nina. "This person helped us. She never stopped helping us, no matter how dangerous it was."

My uncle's face reddened. It was his turn to look down at the floor. And that was when I stood up. An idea had been forming in my head ever since my uncle and aunt had asked to see us with the intention of taking us home with them. I had tried to talk about it with Nina, but she had seemed reluctant to hear me out, saying—unconvincingly, I thought—that my uncle and aunt truly only wanted what was best. That idea suddenly solidified into the only decision that made sense, the only decision that felt right for me and my sisters, and the only outcome I believed my parents would have wanted.

"Thank you both for coming to see us today," I said calmly. "And thank you for the offer of going to live with you. It's very generous and kind. But I'm go-

ing to have to say no. I want to stay with our mama."
I looked at Nina when I said this. She nodded ever so
slightly, a sign that furthered my determination.

A moment later, Nadia stood up beside me. "And I
want to stay with our mama."

Then Galya stood. "I want to stay here too."

I looked over at Nina. "That is, if you still want
us."

I could see tears pooling in Nina's eyes. Without
hesitation, she rose from her chair and came over to
us. She gathered Nadia, Galya, and me in a big hug
and then turned to face my uncle and his wife. They
had not budged. They sat, mouths slightly open, staring in disbelief.

Nina smiled a wide, beautiful smile that stretched
across her face and threatened to push past her ears.
Her dimple deepened and her eyes crinkled at the
corners. "As Dina said, I think a decision has been
made," she said. "My girls and I are going to stay
together."

Author's Note

The Nazis invaded Proskurov in July 1941, after which time laws and rules to restrict the freedom of Jewish people were introduced. For the dramatic purpose of this story, and to show how the lives of Ukrainian Jews were affected by the Nazi occupation, I have altered the timeline of events so that the restrictive laws came into effect first, leading up to the invasion.

WHO WAS NINA PUKAS?

It took an incredibly brave and compassionate person to help Jewish people during the Second World War and the Holocaust. The punishment for defying Nazi orders and helping Jews was severe. You could be arrested, imprisoned, shot on the spot, or hanged. Ludviga (Nina) Pukas was one of those heroic people who, despite the danger, was willing to help. It was 1937 when Nina came to the city of Proskurov in Ukraine and got a job as a domestic working for Frima Sternik, a high school teacher who lived with her two daughters, Eldina and Gennadiy.

In 1939, the Second World War began when Adolf Hitler and his Nazi army invaded Poland. Hitler continued his quest to conquer the countries surrounding Germany, and in 1941, the Nazis invaded Ukraine. Frima's home was burned to the ground. She needed to apply for new identity documents, but she knew that as a Jewish woman, she would be targeted. So she decided to register her children as Nina's.

Nina was given a new apartment and, together with Frima and the girls, they moved in. Nina continued to protect and take care of Eldina and Gennadiy even after Frima was arrested and eventually killed. After the war, Nina contacted several relatives of the family. But the girls still regarded Nina as their mother and refused to leave her.

Ludviga Pukas died in 1984 at the age of eighty-two, and in September 1994, she was named Righteous Among the Nations by Yad Vashem in Israel, the highest honor that can be bestowed on a non-Jewish person who saved Jews during the Holocaust.

Nina's story is remarkable for the fact that she was a simple woman who did something extraordinary. By coming to the aid of the Sternik family, she demonstrated moral courage and good citizenship at a dangerous time in history. She was willing to risk her life to help the family she had come to love. The truth is that not enough people were willing to help in the way that Nina did. Had more people stood up to the Nazis and protected more Jews, the outcome of this time in history would have been significantly different. Nina Pukas is a role model for all of us and an example of what is possible.

Kathy Kacer is the author of more than twenty books for young readers. A winner of the Silver Birch, Red Maple, and Jewish Book Awards in Canada and the U.S., Kathy has written unforgettable stories inspired by real events. She lives in Toronto, Ontario.